The Book of Jokes

D1622323

other works by momus

Lusts of a Moron
The Book of Scotlands

Library of Congress Cataloging-in-Publication Data

Momus, 1960-
 The book of jokes / Momus. -- 1st ed.
     p. cm.
 ISBN 978-1-56478-561-9 (pbk. : alk. paper)
 1. Boys--Fiction. 2. Problem families--Fiction. 3. Eccentrics and eccentricities--
Fiction. 4. Farce. I. Title.
 PR6113.O48B66 2009
 823'.92--dc22
                          2009013110

Partially funded by a grant from the Illinois Arts Council, a state agency, and by the
University of Illinois at Urbana-Champaign

www.dalkeyarchive.com

Cover: design and composition by Danielle Dutton, illustrations by Nicholas Motte
Printed on permanent/durable acid-free paper and bound in the United States of
America

The Book of Jokes

a novel by momus

Dalkey Archive Press
Champaign & London

1

It's a snowy night in late June, and milk is spilling from the broken world's murdered head.

I wake up in the glass house. Outside my window lamplighters climb glass ladders and lick the lamps alight. Inside, moths tussle pointlessly in corners.

There's nowhere to hide. Dad darkens my sister's doorway, throws his shadow across the fine-haired skin of her white belly. The lamplighters crane to watch. They will report what they've seen to the postmen, and the postmen will report it to the teachers, and the teachers—solemnly—to their classes. Then the school bullies will corner me in a piss-stinky lavatory cubicle and tell me.

But I'll know already. Because of the taste on Dad's dick.

It happened in the school toilet. Schott and his boys kicked in my cubicle door. They stood there sneering in a circle. My trousers were around my ankles.

"Do you want to die peacefully in your sleep like your grandpa," they asked me, grabbing me and making to push my head down the toilet, "or screaming in terror like his passengers?"

It was a rhetorical question. No, it was a joke.

The joke was a short one, but there was time and space and scenery within it. You could stop inside the joke and delay the punch line for long enough to smoke a cigarette, chat to the other passengers, take a pee, look out the window.

Inside the joke, I stretched out across two seats in my grandfather's coach. The fabric, a blend of rubber and synthetic cloth, was Orlon acrylic fibre. I knew it was called Orlon because my grandad, the driver, had once told me.

The Orlon was comfortable. I could see the top of Grandad's head in the chink between seats. His eyes, visible in the rearview mirror, were still open.

I would leave the joke before the fatal crash, but for now there was no hurry. I felt like a player of video games who abandons the action-packed plot and just wanders around looking at polygonal trees in peaceful, bitmapped parks filled with sampled birdsong.

"How are you doing?" I called across the aisle to a mother and her plump daughter.

"Very well, thank you," said the mother, a little stiffly. Her daughter gave me a bulgy-eyed stare.

I started daydreaming. I dreamed of shepherds playing panpipes, of Scottish Expressionist paintings, of golf courses and stables and Edith Sitwell. I began to feel drowsy, but quickly jolted alert. It was vital I didn't fall asleep in the middle of the joke. If I slept I would die.

I turned to the mother and daughter. The mother was producing cucumber sandwiches from a plastic box.

"I'm the grandson of the bus driver," I called above the drone of my grandfather's engine.

"Ah," mouthed the mother, "very nice!"

"The grandson of the man driving this joke . . ."

But my words were drowned out by the revving engine. We swung around a particularly treacherous corner. My grandfather ground into low gear.

The plump little girl grabbed a mirror built into a compact case containing orangey-pink foundation powder and lifted it to the window. I knew the game: with the mirror held to one eye and angled forward at forty-five degrees to the glass, you could imagine you were sitting in the cockpit of a pointed vehicle rushing into an exhilaratingly symmetrical landscape. I'd done the same at her age.

But she would never live to be my age. She was in a joke involving a coach crash. I wondered whether to broach the subject, to warn the passengers, to alert my grandfather. Should I feed him coffee from the thermos flask I knew he kept in his military canvas bag?

Then again, what was the point? This version of my grandfather only existed to crash his bus in this joke. The entire landscape was synthetic; everyone and everything here had been created for a laugh. There would be other chances to meet my grandfather, in other jokes.

I glanced again at Gramps's eyes in the rearview mirror. They were drooping, closing. In a few seconds the bus would mount the hard shoulder, explode through the safety barrier and jackknife—slowly, slowly—into the jagged ravine. It was time to leave.

Raucous laughter rang around the stinky toilet. I didn't smile.

"He doesn't get it," shouted Ben Nelson, Schott's loyal lieutenant.

"He's gonna get it all right," said Schott.

2

My name is Sebastian Skeleton. This is my prison diary.

In the exercise yard today I heard two men arguing about whether it's possible for two men to be each other's uncles.

"Of course it is," said one (a child molester).

"No it isn't," said the other (a murderer).

"Look, it's possible for a man to have an uncle, right?" said the Molester.

"Of course it is, I'm not disputing that," answered the Murderer.

"Then all I have to prove to you is that a man could have an uncle who was also his nephew."

"And how could that be?" the Murderer demanded.

"Because he would be an uncle via one union, and a nephew via another."

The murderer, who wasn't very bright, was quiet for a while as he tried to work out in his head whether this was possible or not.

"I need a piece of paper," he said.

The Molester walked over to a blank stretch of wall and picked up a sharp stone. He began scratching a complicated family diagram on the dark concrete.

"Look," the Molester said, "here's one family. And here's another. Here's me in the middle."

"All right," said the Murderer.

"Now, my uncle is my mum's brother, right?"

"All right," said the Murderer. "That's your uncle. Your mum's brother."

"But he's also my nephew," continued the Molester.

"How?"

"Because I'm his dad's brother."

"You can't be his dad's brother!"

"Why not?"

"Because he's your mum's brother!"

"What's that got to do with it?" demanded the Molester.

It was beginning to rain. I walked out of earshot for a couple of minutes and gazed at a chemical refinery on the horizon. Tiny flames burned atop steel chimneys, reflected in the mysterious domed structures grouped nearby. It was something I looked at every day, something that filled me with optimism.

When I came back, the men were still talking.

The Murderer seemed confused. "You can't be his mum's . . . his dad's brother because . . . you can't be that old."

"Why can't I be that old?" demanded the Molester.

"Because you've got to be young enough to be the son of his sister," insisted the Murderer.

"She's old, very old, his sister," said the Molester. "She had me when she was very young. Then her parents had him when she was very old. There's enough space there to fit two generations if the fucking starts nice and early, know what I mean?"

"You fucking pervert," said the Murderer, glancing at me then back at the Molester, "you should have been strangled at birth."

"Strangled? You're a horrible murderer, you are," said the Molester, also looking at me, then back at his friend the Murderer. "When it comes to people like you, the death penalty should be a pre-emptive strike. But, to get back to the matter at hand, you have to admit that in this instance I'm right. Two men can be each other's uncles."

"I don't see it," said the Murderer, crinkling his ruddy, cliffy brow. His inability to grasp the problem was getting him seriously rattled.

"Okay, let me spell it out for you, Einstein," said the Molester. "Say I'm forty. My mum—who's my uncle's sister, remember—is fifty-five. She had me when she was fifteen."

The Murderer looked disgusted. "Go on," he said.

"So when I was fifteen, how old was my mum?"

The Murderer thought. "She was thirty, of course."

"Correct. And a filthy slut she was. And a right looker. So I fucked her. Nine months later she had my uncle. His name was Brian. He was fifteen years younger than me, but he was my uncle because he was my mum's brother."

Both men looked at me, then back at each other.

"That's fucking lunacy!" screamed the Murderer. "How could she give birth to her own brother by fucking you? You're a nutter! You need strangling!"

"Wait, wait, I was just testing you!" laughed the Molester, clapping the Murderer on the shoulder. "Just my little joke there. You're right, of course. Brian was born when my mum was thirty. His parents are her parents. Brian and my mum are brother and sister. But here's the beauty bit. Are you ready?"

The Murderer grunted.

"Brian's dad was my mum's brother."

"I'm going to kill you," said the Murderer, looking at me rather than the Molester, "and your whole fucking family."

3

It was a snowy night in late June. My four uncles—The English-man, The Irishman, The Scotsman and The Welshman—were on a hunting trip.

It's extraordinary that four men of such widely different racial backgrounds should be members of the same family, but you must remember that they were born before devolution made those states not only completely independent, but almost terra incognita to one another.

Tell you their names? But I already have. Consult their passports (an English passport, an Irish one, a Scottish and a Welsh one) and you'll see that The Englishman, The Irishman, The Scotsman and The Welshman are their actual and only names. None of them has a "Christian" nor a "family" name.

My uncles, despite enormous differences in racial make-up, cultural habitus, intelligence, national dress and so on, were members of the same family and consequently liked to meet up to celebrate old ties of blood. On such occasions they would typically go hunting, shooting duck on a small island easily accessible from Ireland, Scotland, England and Wales.

One day, on just such a hunting trip, tragedy struck. In the midst of a particularly noisy fusillade, The Englishman crumpled to the ground, apparently felled by a stray burst of buckshot.

The Irishman, The Welshman and The Scotsman gathered around their stricken brother. Lacking my grandfather's callous *sang froid*, they panicked. Each pulled out a mobile telephone and contacted the emergency services of his respective country. In the languages of Scots Gaelic, Irish and Welsh, they explained the situation, each one tripping over the syntax of newly-learned languages reinstated—from conditions of near-oblivion—since independence.

"Wrong-thing with shooting-stick! Brother lying ground!" is the literal translation of The Welshman's explanation of the accident to the major Cardiff hospital whose number he had stored in his machine.

"Bang! Bang! Dead! Human not duck!" explained the Scotsman to a hospital receptionist in the Mount Florida district of Glasgow.

"Man bite ground, probably dead!" was The Irishman's stumbling attempt, flashed via satellite to Emergency Services in Dublin.

"Now, sir, calm down," came the reply, over all three phones, to all three men. "We'd better use English. The first thing to do is make sure your friend is really dead."

There came three loud bangs—one, two, a short delay filled with horror, and then a third (The Irishman). "Done!" chorused the uncles. "Now what?"

As the rumours and innuendo spread, school became increasingly unbearable for me. Often, instead of going to class, I'd squeeze through a small hole in a fence near the bus stop and climb the steep wooded slope that led to the deerpark.

Why was there a deerpark on top of this small suburban mountain? I don't know. The site felt like it must have contained a great country house at some point, but all that was left was a clearing in a forest on the top of a hill, seemingly inaccessible by any official driveway, path, or stair. The only occupiers were a few terrified deer and the occasional peacock.

At the top of the hill there were some spider-infested outhouses, and a scattering of nineteenth-century rubble laid out in the vague shape of foundations. On my truancy days I'd come here to be alone and smoke. I'd watch the drizzle soaking into the moss, and stare down deer as they peeked out at me from behind damp trees, shivering.

One day—it was a late afternoon in early winter, and already getting dark—I ground my last cigarette butt underfoot in the grey putty path of the ruined greenhouse and made my way back to the forest, and the steep slope that led home.

My descent was cut short by a sinister man wearing a clown outfit.

"Hello, little boy," he said.

"Hello."

"Why are you so scared?" he demanded, with a queer, strangled laugh.

I wasn't scared at all, really, just surprised to see such a ridiculous pantomime horror figure in the middle of this forest. I said nothing.

I had nothing to fear from the clown; his sole purpose was to deliver a stupid, menacing punchline, tug down his flies, and make people laugh at my expense. He had no more lines, no role beyond that, no function, no further dimensions. He didn't even have a penis under his fly. He was a shill, a plant, a stuffed shirt, a cypher.

"Why are you so scared," repeated the clown, unzipping his fly, "when I'm the one who's going to have to walk back through this forest alone?"

And, crinkling his red and white face into a thousand creases, he trilled a stark, screaming, ridiculous, deciduous laugh.

I walked around him and—sure enough—the clown was quite flat, a rigid piece of card propped up by splints. I kicked at him from behind and he fell forwards slowly, landing face down on the muddy forest floor.

Like a damp spermy condom, a used character from a joke is something pathetic and sad, the kind of thing you find abandoned in a forest whose trees are draped with polythene bags.

I walked back through the forest alone.

I am writing this down late at night, in my room upstairs at the glass house. The walls give me a clear view of the forest beside our house, my lamp, the nearby hill. If I dim the screen of my computer a bit I can see a jet climbing away from the airport twenty kilometers away. Soon it will be light. Perhaps the passengers on that plane can already see the top of the sun.

4

I came face to face with the Murderer and the Molester in the prison refectory. They were hated men, but they hated me more. My crimes were twice as bad as theirs. Twice as bad as both of theirs put together, I mean. They were going to kill me. Both of them. Twice.

My only chance was to tell them a story.

"I have the answer to your conundrum, gentlemen," I began. "The one I heard you discussing in the yard."

Silence.

"Bill has sex with his mother to produce Mike, Bill's son . . . and also his brother."

The Murderer looked blank, but The Molester broke a gappy smile.

"Go on," he said.

"Mike has a daughter, Ava. She's Bill's grand-daughter and also his niece."

"Who fucks her?" demanded the leering Molester. He had a pimple on his nose.

The Murderer laughed and made a strangling gesture around the Molester's neck.

I swallowed and said: "Her grandad."

"What?"

"Her grandad, he fucks her. Mike's dad Jake."

"Nice and slow and hard," says the Molester, his eyes squeezed tight. "On her eleventh birthday."

"I'm warning you," says the Murderer. "And you" (to me). "Doesn't nobody get killed in this story?"

"Not in this story, no," I reply, smoothly, soothingly. "But next time . . ."

"All right, make it quick, then. Her grandad fucks Ava."

"Yes, Jake fucks Ava good . . . good and slow, when she's . . . young . . . very young."

Both men's eyes are on me, glittering. They're listening, filthy.

"Nine months later, Ava has Sid, a little boy."

"Pittocks! Bumfluff!" spits the Murderer. "She's only eleven! Don't you know nothing about biology?"

"Shut up," says the Molester. "Some women are utterly fertile at eleven. I've known it 'appen. I've known 'em. 'Ad 'em an' all."

"She might have been a little older, I can't remember," I said. "Grandad Jake crept up to her room for, oh, years."

"So anyway," I carried on, "Sid is born into the world. Sid is Mike's great-grandson, his grand-nephew, and also his uncle."

"See, you halfwitted imbecile," said the Molester, turning to the Murderer, "I told you it was possible."

"You asserted it was possible," corrected the Murderer, "but you were unable to tell me how. That's because you're a fuckwit. This gent has made it all perfectly clear. I tip my hat to him."

Both men beamed at me.

I went to take a pee. The urinal had a comfortingly acrid smell; the urine of badly-fed, embittered men mixed with the antiseptic stink of disinfectant buoys. I loved the sound of water gurgling in the pipes—it was my favourite kind of music. There was a flat, high, distant, white sound, a bubbling foreground sound, a ventilation drone, the sound of a moth skittering against the fluorescent tube above, and the very faint sound of two types of wind—the clean kind eddying around outside, and the dirty kind escaping my own body.

5

It snowed and it snowed. My father was playing chess with his penis.

He'd set up a low table and two stools by the glass wall that faced the garden. His penis sat on one stool, its back to the window. My father, who was the more patient of the two, was playing with care and skill, but the penis—a hothead—played all sorts of wild and risky moves. For the moment, they were paying off.

A log fire crackled in the grate . . . But wait, before I tell you about that, I must provide a little background.

Before the glass house, before the city, before hysterical males came to dominate our family, we lived in a farmhouse set in an orchard. Those were days of fruit and blossom, the days when my mother was still with us. This is the story of how she came to leave.

Sebastian Skeleton, my father, was not, in those days, the priapic monster he has since become. He was a relatively sensitive man, a horticulturalist, a maker of thin-lipped pottery with his own hand-built kiln, an avid reader of insipidly nationalistic poetry written in the Finno-Ugrian family of languages. Unfortunately, he was also having an affair. And even more unfortunately, it was with a barnyard fowl.

Where did the sordid tryst between the goose and my father begin? How did the witless bird inspire his love, and what were the feathery guiles she employed to make him lose interest so completely in my mother?

It's difficult to answer these questions. What seems certain is that the location of the goose shed next to the fragile structure housing my father's pottery kiln provided him with the perfect alibi.

It was I, Peter, who found the secret interconnecting door, bent low to pass through it, and saw the two suspicious concaves in the straw—recent, warm impressions of the bodies of man and goose. Scraping around next to them, I also found a foul pile of goose eggs. I took them to the pig pen and tossed them in, wincing as I watched greedy Pippi snout them open and guzzle their spilled contents—failed amalgams, no doubt, of human and goose.

I am reminded of a similar case of a rural man wracked by sexual desires he couldn't—or wouldn't—control. I discovered, in my father's bookcase, the diary of the typographer, sculptor and artist Eric Gill. One day in 1929 he noted in his diary:

"Bath. Continued experiment with dog after and discovered that a dog will join with a man."

Fuck!

We can imagine my father's journal striking a similar tone. "Bath. After, discovered that a goose will join with a man."

But what of my mother? She certainly didn't deserve my father's neglect. She was a woman as well-endowed with intelligence as with beauty. She must have had an inkling of what was going on. Perhaps she noticed how my father had stopped eating paté, once his favourite food.

Anyway, whatever triggered her suspicion, soon after my father's affair with the goose began, my mother returned from her regular charity work in the local village with a fine spruce gander. My father, of course, immediately saw the bird as a dangerous rival.

"Take it back," he demanded, "we don't need any more geese on this farm!"

My mother explained that the gander would keep Rebecca—our goose—company, and help her produce handsome goslings that we could sell at market. My father protested, but finally (in order not to look suspicious) had to accept the fowl, who was christened Emperor and given free range of the barnyard.

A mere two weeks later Emperor was found with his neck rung. My father blamed foxes, but what fox rings the neck of a goose and fails to take a single bite of its flesh? Later, I discovered an account of the murder in his secret diary. Emperor had plunged my father into the depths of depression—a depression fuelled by jealousy.

"I wish only to die," he had written. "Bring me an undertaker who will sell me a plot! For I have surprised my mistress in the arms—or should I say the wings?—of her husband, the gander Emperor. I thought I was happy, and had love at the end of my harpoon . . ." (such was my father's odd, florid, antique style of writing) ". . . but yesterday evening, at the corner of the wood, I came upon my mistress copulating with her husband. What treachery!"

"This so-called emperor of the barnyard, this humping, preening feathered camel, cock of the walk, how can I find the words to describe my disgust for him?" continued my father, rage carrying his metaphors to hell in a handcart. "In beguiling his own wife to cheat on her lover with him, he has taken adultery to its logical conclusion. I had noticed that the embraces of her beak were less fierce upon my lips than before. It is all due to him, her husband! Now she will make offspring who no longer resemble me."

(My father seems to have become feverish at this point—the goose had made no human-shaped offspring, nor could she.)

"I have surprised the geese," my father continued, "at the corner of the wood! And just to rub it in, the imperial gander is now squawking his taunts around the barnyard—the one who is wearing the cuckold's horns, he says, isn't the one you think! How he hisses his derision, how he mocks me! He will die for this humiliation! I shall ring Emperor's neck tonight!"

The next entry is curt. "Rang Emperor's neck. I shall tell them a fox did it. Afterwards, crept away to Rebecca's shed. She rejected me. I forced her. The bitch is only a goose. She should not forget it. Nor, for that matter, remember it."

And there you see, pithily summed up, my father's insufferable character, the double binds he would force on all those he came into contact with. We could neither be what we were—innocent children, deserving of protection—nor his lovers, his mates, his equals, as we also longed to be.

As for his wife, our mother, his callous attitude to her is clear.

Holding the goose Rebecca under his arm, my father strode into the farmhouse kitchen. "This is the pig I've been fucking," he declared. My mother looked up, surprised. "That's not a pig, that's Rebecca the goose!" "I wasn't talking to you," snapped my father.

My mother fled. She packed her bags one day and left us, never to return. My father smashed all his pottery and burned down the barn with Rebecca still in it. We moved to the city, to the glass house, where, in full view of the lamplighters, my father now sits playing chess.

"Checkmate," says my father's penis.

6

It's me, Sebastian. I'm in the prison toilets, in the middle cubicle, listening to the beautiful sounds of the pipes as I squeeze one out.

Suddenly I hear the voices of the Murderer and the Molester. The Murderer is in the cubicle on my right, the Molester in the cubicle on my left. They're having a conversation.

"Blood," said the Murderer.

"What's that?" called the Molester, "Blood in your stool?"

"Nah, it all depends on blood. The uncle problem."

They were still talking about the uncle problem.

"Everything's about blood for you," drawled the Molester, "that's why you're a murderer by trade."

"Blood is cleaner than sperm," returned the Murderer. "Everybody hates a molester. Anyway, as I was saying, the uncle doesn't have to be a blood uncle."

"A blood uncle, what's that, something like a blood orange?" asked the Molester. "A juicy uncle with a blood-red hue? Sounds like you!"

"I mean, he doesn't have to be a your-dad's-brother type of uncle, just an uncle by marriage, like the husband of your mum's sister."

"Ah well, that's easy, innit," said the Molester. "Much too easy. If my uncle's just the husband of my mum's sister, all I have to do to become his uncle is marry his mum's sister and—Bob's your uncle, Hugh—he's my uncle."

"You want something a bit more intimate, don't you, Christian?" came the Murderer's voice, mingled with the sound of crisp, sharp paper being scrunched up a fundament. "You want some of the old incest, dontcha? Because you're a molester, intcha, Christian?"

The Molester sounded a hurt-yet-dignified note. "Perhaps I am. It just strikes me as a more inherently elegant solution, that's all."

"In'erently helligant? Wot?" said the Murderer.

"Listen," said the Molester, and flushed his toilet.

"Wot?" ejaculated the Murderer, muffled in the double rush, flushing his own pan too.

"The simplest, best and most elegant solution is this. Dad has sex with his own daughter."

"Good, hard and slow," added the Murderer, who was staying in his cubicle for some reason.

"Yes, good hard and slow," agreed the Molester, who was also staying in his.

I crouched where I was, afraid the slightest movement would give me away.

"Nine months later," continued the voice on my left, "the little girl has twins, two lovely little boys. They're both their mother's brother as well as her son, so they're each other's uncles."

"And when they're old enough to make spunk," said the Murderer, his breath coming in fits and starts, "they fuck their little mother and she has two more sons who are . . ."

". . . the uncles of their uncles' uncles!" I shouted, and flushed my toilet.

As the water subsided and the tank refilled, silence descended over the cubicles.

"I do believe there's a snake in the grass," said the Murderer.

"I'm going to kill you and your entire family," said the Molester, staring down at me from the gap between the cubicle wall and the ceiling. His disheveled hair and lurid face made me start back in fear. "What's your address?"

I told him.

"I'm going to kill you and your entire family," he stressed, "and I know your address."

7

It seems that my uncle The Englishman was much better loved—and better placed—than any of us had imagined. At his funeral there were enough people—respectable people, powerful people, the great and the good, all dressed up in bobbing floral hats and formal coats-and-tails—to fill the small cathedral of the provincial English town in which he was raised.

My uncle had left very specific instructions regarding his funeral. He wanted a valedictory oration from Brother Francesco, a monk—the best, the kindest, the most generous soul, The Englishman said, he'd had the good fortune to encounter on his travels. There was just one problem. Since their last meeting, and unbeknownst to The Englishman, Brother Francesco had suffered a terrible injury.

It happened, in a sense, because of the very qualities my uncle had remarked upon. Francesco was a kind and trusting man, and his nature communicated itself quickly to all the living creatures he encountered, men and animals alike, taming and charming even the most savage among them.

The monk liked to climb hills, seeking out high and solitary places from which to contemplate the perfection of God's creation. In a copse in the foothills of an Umbrian mountain he was surprised one afternoon by a bear. Others would have fled or plugged the beast with a musket, but Francesco had more powerful weapons: his faith, his charm and his trust. Soon he and the bear were fast friends. Returning day after day to the same spot beneath a magnificent cedar tree, Francesco and the bear developed a deep mutual love, respect and trust. Unable to talk, they nevertheless pledged, by certain signs and gestures, an oath of mutual protection.

Alas, the bear was all too true to his promise. When Brother Francesco happened to fall asleep and a bee landed on his forehead, the bear—seeing an affront—picked up a rock and smashed it down on the sleeping monk's head. The tiny intruder was crushed, certainly, but so too were significant portions of Francesco's brain.

As the officiating minister at The Englishman's funeral explained to the assembled congregation, the monk had survived, but now suffered from a strange and awkward mental impairment: Francesco always spoke the approximate opposite of what he intended to say.

When news of The Englishman's death—and the request in his will—had reached the hospital where the monk was being treated, hasty attempts had been made to coach and coax him to say only bad things about The Englishman, so that they would come out good. But the benign monk had curtly refused: "If I didn't believe The Englishman to have been the biggest fucking bastard who ever walked God's earth," he proclaimed, "I wouldn't say it!"

He meant, of course, that since he did believe The English-man to have been a saint, this—and this alone—is what he would tell the congregation at the funeral. Unfortunately, the poor man had no understanding of his condition, and even less grasp of how to correct it. The very notion of insincerity—even with the very best of intentions—was abhorrent to him.

The organisers of the funeral had therefore decided to let Brother Francesco conduct his oration in his own way, with the proviso that his peculiar and unfortunate condition would be explained to the congregation beforehand. In a brief pref-ace the explanation was given—the tale of the bear and the bee and the brain damage. A buzz passed through the gen-teel crowd, a ripple of anxiety. Francesco ascended slowly and painfully to the pulpit lectern clothed in simple brown robes gathered at the waist with a knotted cord.

"The Englishman," he began, his voice swelling with emo-tion, "was the sourest double-dealing ratfink—the smallest-hearted wretch—I never did know. How I hated this woman, the worst that ever died!"

It went on this way for quite some time, with worsening language and to growing consternation in the crowd—as well as some desperate, dark giggling, suppressed with bolts of Kleenex. Even the monk seemed to sense that it was all com-ing out wrong. At last, with tears streaming down his face, he reached his heartfelt conclusion: "This mean, evil, utterly sin-ister buttfuck of a motherfucker—my worst enemy—is even now, I most feebly hope, flailing, with farcical cowardice, at the left hand of His Majesty the Devil," he cried.

"Bad riddance to a small and repulsive creep!"

There were gasps, and some "amens," from the crowd. The man on my right turned and introduced himself as Francesco's speech therapist. "It's utterly remarkable," he whispered, "he's made a complete recovery!"

As I prepared to leave I noticed my neighbours on the left. Their outfits—wide hats netted at the brim, full-body polyester suits and stout leather gloves—marked them out as beekeepers. They were talking about bees, squooshing spurts of sweetly-scented smoke into the air from small green cans.

"It's always a mistake, killing bees," said the First Beekeeper.

"Never leads to anything good," agreed the Second. "How many do you tend?"

"I've got two thousand bees in five hives," said the First. "What about you?"

"I've got thirty thousand bees in two hives," replied the Second.

"Thirty thousand bees in just two hives?" exclaimed the First. "Isn't that a bit much?"

"Fuck 'em," said the Second, "they're only bees."

8

The men cornered me by the wash-basins. This wasn't supposed to happen. I was supposed to have been spared all forms of assault. I was supposed to have charmed my way out of it. I was Scheherazade, the weaver of tales, the prisoner who'd outlive and outlast all the . . .

"Grab his cock!" shouted the Murderer.

The Molester tipped me back over the basin, gripping the underside of my chin and shoving me towards the cracked mirror. My spine was at an excruciating angle, my head crunched into the glass.

"Oh dear, cracked the mirror," said the Murderer, sarcastically. "We wouldn't want Mr Skeleton taking a shard of broken glass home to his cell and using it as a dagger, would we?"

"He might do himself some serious harm with a shard of broken glass," agreed the Molester. "He might plunge it into his sensitive stomach, or sever an artery and lack, at the crucial moment, for a tourniquet."

"Lack for a tourniquet," chuckled the Murderer, "I've seen a few slip away for want of those."

"'Ow many?" gurned the Molester.

"Gentlemen," I shouted out, struggling for my life, "I told you I had another tale to tell you!"

"Oh really, Skeleton?" said the Murderer. "And of what might your lay treat? Make it good, or we'll hee-viscerate yer horgans!"

The time had come.

"I shall relate my crimes," I said.

The two men stood back. I straightened up, swept a strand of bloody hair out of my eyes, and tugged my prison jacket back into shape.

9

You might think that, after the episode with the goose, my mother—whose name was Joan—would have no further contact with my father. But that was not the case. In fact, when we moved to the glass house, she also moved to the city, occupying a house nearby shaped like an enormous whisky bottle. (Our neighbourhood, known for its bizarre architectural follies, was quite a tourist draw.)

My mother, who had always been a bisexual, began an affair with another woman, also called Joan. Joan and Joan looked strikingly alike. They began to dress alike, and soon were almost impossible to tell apart. We children used to visit often, and soon we discovered that the other Joan had moved in with our mother.

Unfortunately, we were not the only ones to visit. My father struck up a friendship with my mother's lesbian lover, and began making secret visits to the whisky-bottle house.

Absurdly enough, in the course of these visits, he never told Joan that he had once been the other Joan's husband. For her, he was simply a kind, amusing and well-endowed man who enjoyed humping with her when her lover was out. My mother, apparently wishing to erase my father from her life altogether, had never spoken of her marriage, nor described her ex-husband in any way. He who is ignorant of history, they say, is condemned to repeat it, and this is what Joan now began to do.

My father, tiring of the risks associated with meeting his new lover in the whisky-bottle house, began to invite her to the old country farmhouse, which he still owned. The place had got a little run-down—especially the kitchen, which sorely lacked a woman's touch—but essentially it was as we had left it. Except, obviously, for the fact that some of the outhouses had been burned down.

Imagine my father's surprise when, making love with the second Joan one day in the farmhouse bedroom, he saw silhouetted in the window, cameoed against an enormous harvest moonrise, the unmistakable outline of Rebecca, his goose lover!

But how could this be? Had he not destroyed the seductive bird by burning down her barn? Was this, then, her ghost, back from the ashes to haunt him?

With all the hairs on his body standing erect, but disguising his agitation with a few casual words to Joan, who lay naked on the mattress, my father went outside to investigate.

There in the blazing moonlight there could be no doubt—it was indeed Rebecca! The way the skin was formed on her pink legs, the cow-lick fluff of her impossibly soft cream-coloured underbelly—this could be no other bird! And she had not lost one feather of her charm!

My father's absence was long, and the naked Joan grew restless. When he returned, he made up some foolish excuse—the moon, shining through a magnifying glass, had set a small bale of hay on fire, he said, and he had been obliged to put it out.

In reality it was something else he was extinguishing: his lust for a gorgeous goose he had thought long dead, destroyed by his own hand. And, in the course of the next few weeks, he would extinguish this lust over and over, making use of a warm, dark corner of a tractor garage filled with a shabby pile of oiled rags.

When he returned to the neglected Joan smelling of sperm, paté, motor oil and goose down, my father could not help but arouse the lady's suspicions. Soon his desire for pretence grew threadbare. Joan's worst fears were confirmed when, one evening, my father strode into the farmhouse kitchen with Rebecca under his arm and declared, "This is the pig I've been fucking!"

"But darling," said Joan, "that's not a pig, that's a goose!"

"I wasn't talking to you," snapped my father.

Joan packed her bags and took the next train back to the city. She decided to make a clean breast of her transgression to Joan, her lesbian lover.

"Joan, my darling," she said, "I cannot hide this any longer. I have been betraying your trust . . . with a man."

And in fits, spurts and flurries of tears the sorry tale came out. She described their trysts in the farmhouse, and the strange scene earlier in the evening with the goose.

My mother listened with mounting recognition and rising bile. When Joan came to the end of her story and fell to her knees to beg Joan for forgiveness, Joan granted it immediately.

"I can forgive you," she said, "as I have forgiven myself. But I shall never forgive him—the father of my children!"

And Joan gasped as, for the first time, Joan told her the whole story of her marriage. By the time she reached the end, both Joans were hissing with hatred for my father. Such duplicity! Such two-facedness! Such double-dealing!

The two ladies resolved to exact the ultimate revenge. Joan would dress up as Joan and surprise my father in the garage in the act of copulation with Rebecca. Then the second Joan would appear, take the first Joan in her arms, and say, "This is the pig I've been fucking."

When my father inevitably began to expostulate, stammering "That's not a pig, that's Joan!" both Joans would shout in unison "I wasn't talking to you!"

Then, quickly spreading petrol around the garage, they would set it alight and burn it down, making sure that my father was trapped inside with the goose.

They executed the plan the very next night. Sure enough, there was my father, in the garage, naked on his hands and knees, grunting disgustingly as he penetrated the nether regions of the goose.

"This is the pig I've been fucking," shouted Joan. My father whipped around.

"I'm not a pig!" he exclaimed.

"I wasn't talking to you!" said Joan, who by now had been joined by the other Joan (their timing wasn't quite perfect—they were running behind schedule). "I was talking to Joan!"

"But this isn't Joan," said my father, pointing to the goose. "This is Rebecca!"

10

The Murderer and the Molester were gazing at me with rounded eyes. A leaky tap dripped and the urinals squittered.

"Come on, then!" they said. "What did you do? What landed you in here?"

"I'll tell you," I said. "But first I want you to agree to something."

"What's that?" asked the men.

"I want you to agree to help me to escape from this place. For us all to help each other to escape from this place."

"How can we do that?" asked the Murderer. "This is a high-security prison. We all committed serious crimes."

"There are ways," I said. "The private security staff they use . . . that's the weak spot in the system. There are other ways too . . . I've been studying them."

"Well, you're the smart one, Professor," said the Murderer. "If anyone's got the intelligence what can get us out of here, it's you. So"—he glanced at the Molester—"I think we should go with the Prof, eh, Scotty?"

"That's not my name," said the Molester tetchily.

"So we swear to execute a plan to get out?" I demanded. "Shall we swear it here and now in blood?"

"Not blood, too suspicious, DNA," said the Murderer.

"Okay, just a verbal contract between us," I said. "But sworn on the thing we each hold most sacred. And we have to say what that is."

The Murderer and the Molester looked at each other.

"All right," said the Murderer. "I swear by murder itself to help us three to escape from this slammer."

"My turn," said the Molester. "I swear by molestation itself—molestation most delirious, in all its sundry forms!—to be loyal to you two and to bear my part of the burden of work that will, eventually, I believe, ensure the success of our escape."

Both men turned to me. I couldn't really demand any more from them. They had sworn by what they held most sacred.

"And what do you swear by?" they demanded.

"Wait, before I tell you that—before I swear by the crime I committed, as you have sworn by yours—I must add an important condition."

The men waited to hear.

"My condition is this. That, should our escape be a success, we must go directly, as soon as we're free, and actually commit the crimes that landed us here in prison."

There was uproar in the bathroom. Both men started shouting. Two screws burst in and clanged their night sticks against the pipes on either side of the door.

"Shut up! Shut up you three!" the screws shouted. "Now, who started this rumpus?"

I pointed at the Murderer, the Murderer pointed at the Molester, and the Molester pointed at me.

11

My mother, Joan, ran into financial difficulties soon after setting up house with her lesbian lover, Joan. But Joan, my mother's lover, came up with an ingenious way to earn a living.

Joan opened a bank account and soon began stashing away quite large amounts of money in it. One day, she set up a meeting to get financial advice. "But it has to be from the manager of the bank himself," she insisted. The bank agreed (the sums going into her account made her, after all, one of their most important customers).

Sitting face-to-face with the manager, Joan said "I've come for financial advice."

"Your account seems very healthy," said the bank manager. "Thousands of euros are flowing through it. Do you mind my asking the source of your income?"

"Bets," said Joan. "I bet on things."

"Really?" said the manager. "What kind of things?"

"Well, quite unlikely things, which I think, nevertheless, are going to happen. High-stake bets, with high returns."

"For instance . . . ?"

"Well, for instance, I predict that by ten o'clock tomorrow morning your testicles will be cubic."

The manager spluttered. "My testicles will be cubic? My dear lady, that's a little far-fetched, isn't it? How can you win any money at all if that's the kind of thing you're betting on?"

"Are you really so sure it's impossible? Then accept my challenge! I bet you €10,000 that at ten o'clock tomorrow morning you'll have cubic testicles. If you think you won't, put your money where your mouth is!"

Challenged in this way, the bank manager couldn't refuse. "Very well," he said. "Let's meet here again at ten tomorrow morning."

That night, at home, the bank manager rolled down his trousers and pants in front of the mirror and examined himself before retiring to bed. His testicles were definitely rounded, as before. Just to make sure, he cupped them in his hands. Nothing was irregular there—or, rather, nothing was too regular, too oblong. He would win the bet.

And, speculating on how he'd generously return the €10,000 to the eccentric lady immediately on winning the bet, then give her some proper financial advice, the bank manager drifted off to sleep.

He had a horrific dream. His testicles had swollen to several times their normal size. Two junior managers were kneeling before him, measuring the abnormal growth. They looked like old Polish tailors.

"Measure twice, cut once," chorused the two juniors, fingering the manager's balls.

"All right," said the manager, "get on with it."

"Your testicles have inflated at six times the bank's standard compound interest rate," exclaimed the juniors, "outstripping inflation. Shall we cut the percentage?"

And they swished two shaving razors through the air, setting a grey cloud of pubic hair a-fluttering.

"No!" cried the bank manager, "cut nothing until we have received the central bank's mortgage lending-rate adjustments!"

At that moment there was a hammering at the door. Two heralds entered, flat as playing cards, blew on Japanese silver tofu trumpets, and announced a proclamation from the central bank. There was to be no adjustment to the lending rate, but all bank managers were required to have their balls boxed, by a sort of bonsai process, into cubes. A terrifying gardener, wearing several layers of brown aprons and bright red rubber gloves, approached. Strapped to his clumped fists were two great wooden cymbals. Clapped together, the wooden lids made the clacking sound of kabuki hand drums.

"Prepare your balls for boxing!" shouted the gardener.

The manager woke up trembling. It was morning, and the sheets were clammy and twisted. He groaned, rushed over to the full-length mirror, and examined his testicles. They were small and rounded, perfectly normal apart from the fact that fear had made them gird themselves slightly higher than usual in their sacs.

After his shower, the manager dressed with particular care, selecting his best pair of underpants and steaming and creasing them in his Corby Press before pulling them on. Thus equipped, he set off for the bank slightly earlier than was his habit.

Joan was waiting for him with Bernard Bernardson, the lawyer. Joan wore a double-girded chiton and a himation in diplax configuration. Bernard Bernardson wore a yellow chiton draped with a splendid purple peplos and kilted above the knee.

"I'd like you to meet Bernard Bernardson, my lawyer," said Joan. "He's here to see that our agreement is honoured and all the conditions of the bet fulfilled."

"Very well," said the bank manager. "But I can tell you straight away that no change has occurred to my testicles."

"Well, that is what we must now ascertain," said Joan. "As you can see, the hour of ten is now just minutes away. Shall we enjoy the privacy of your office?"

The party stepped into the bank manager's office.

"I wonder if you would be so kind as to disrobe," said Joan. "You needn't remove jacket, waistcoat, shirt or tie, just the bottom half."

"Of course," said the bank manager. He dropped his pants and tried clumsily to pull the legs over his big black patent leather shoes. It was impossible, so he took the large black shoes off. Soon he stood in his neatly-pressed underpants, faintly scented with lavender.

"And the underpants," insisted Joan, "those must also be removed, for the sake of clarity".

The manager complied, slipping the cotton down his lightly-haired legs. Soon his testicles were entirely exposed, seething uneasily in the air-conditioning like a beached pink sea anemone.

"So you see, madam," said the bank manager, eager to be over with the proof, "my testicles are not cubic. They remain perfectly normal."

"I'm afraid I must ask you to permit me to feel them with my hand," said Joan.

"Is it strictly necessary?" asked the manager.

"It is."

"Very well."

Joan stepped forward, fixed the bank manager with a steely gaze, and gave his testicles a tight squeeze. The manager winced.

"And?" he demanded.

"As you say, they are quite normal," declared Joan. "I have lost the bet."

And she handed the relieved bank manager a block of green paper containing one hundred hundred-euro notes.

The lawyer Bernard Bernardson began to bang his head against the wall.

The naked bank manager handed the €10,000 back to Joan. "I have won the bet, but I ask you to take your money back, my dear lady," he said, raising his voice over the banging sound. "I shall not exploit such an excellent customer."

"That is gracious indeed," shouted Joan, pocketing the cash.

"What is your lawyer doing?" demanded the bank manager, pulling his underpants and trousers back on. Bernard Bernardson had cut his head and was bleeding slightly onto the wallpaper, which bore the bank's insignia in blue and white.

"Bernard is upset," said Joan. "You see, the other day he bet me €20,000 that I wouldn't be able to touch your balls."

12

Prisoners used to work sewing mail bags, but these days you're more likely to be dealing with customer complaints in a call centre. Nobody knows—when they ring up to complain about a missing package or a delay in their new passport arriving—that the voice on the other end of the phone belongs to a prisoner.

The Murderer, the Molester and I all sat next to each other in the octagonal room, under the skylights, facing flat-screen monitors, headsets clamped over our ears. It was tough work dipping into databases, trying to remain cool, collected and courteous. Angry customers swore like . . . well, like hardened lags in jail.

The shift ended at 7 P.M. I eased a tirading male to as natural an end as I could manage. All calls, incidentally, are monitored for quality control purposes.

"I'm very sorry about this, sir," I said, "and I can assure you that we take this failure very seriously and will try our utmost to ensure that your passport will be issued at the earliest opportunity. All right, sir?"

"I'm going to kill you and your entire family," said the man, and hung up.

The Murderer and the Molester were waiting for me in the stairwell.

"You said you'd tell us about your crimes," said the Molester. "We can't trust you until we hear what they are."

"Yes," said the Murderer, "now's the time. Speak."

"All right," I said, "just stand back and let me speak."

They stood back.

"I molested a young girl," I said.

"Go on."

"On my walk home from work I noticed a room that was lit on winter evenings. You couldn't help seeing that it was a young girl's bedroom. One evening, on impulse, I saw she was there, sitting before a mirror. I looked behind and ahead. The street was empty both ways. I ducked into the garden and took up a position by her window. I watched her for quite a while."

The Molester looked excited. "And?" he said. "That's not a crime. Well, it is, but not much of one."

"It happened several times," I continued. "She was always sitting at her mirror, talking to herself. One evening she came to the window to let the cat out into the garden. I grabbed her wrist and climbed in through the window."

"And?"

"I covered her mouth, led her to the bed, made her . . . do things. Bad things, dirty things, degrading things. She hardly complained at all. Her mother started calling. I dashed out through the window, zipping up as I stumbled out. Her dad's car was just coming up the drive. I got caught in the head-lights. The little girl ran out behind me, sperm dribbling from her mouth, shouting. Her dad threw me over the bonnet."

"Here, wait a moment," said the Molester, "that's my crime you're describing! You read about it in the papers, didn't you, you lying bastard? That's what I'm in for!"

I was crestfallen. "Our sort of crime often unfolds in a very similar way," I mumbled, but there was no point pretending.

"You lying cunt," said the Murderer, "that's his crime! Tell us yours!"

"All right," I said. "I killed someone."

"Who?"

"Maybe you read about it in the papers. It was an actress, a soap star, quite well known, lived alone down near the canal. I did it for the jewelry."

The Murderer's eyes bulged.

"You piss-taking runt!" he shouted. "You low, common thief! That's my crime! That's what I'm in for!"

"Many murders begin the same way," I began, but there was no point pretending.

"All right," I said, and sighed heavily. "I'd better tell you the truth. I'm innocent."

The Murderer looked relieved. "So am I," he said.

"Me too," said the Molester, sheepishly.

13

My father and grandfather got on very well. They loved to sit outside a country inn, tugging at the ivy cascading over the walls and drinking iced pastis. And they loved to entertain us children with anecdotes so corrosive to good manners or morals that they made customers sitting at nearby tables blush and rise to leave.

One such story concerned an early expedition my father and grandfather made together to the country. It was my grandfather's day off, but somehow he had the use of his bus and uniform. My father sat in the back seat, buck naked, my grandfather behind the wheel. My father, Sebastian, was masturbating as usual, or rather, whooshing his flexible organ around like a lasso, enjoying the whistling sound it made. My grandfather, meanwhile, was shouting something over his shoulder about the Aeolian harp. It was named after Aeolus, he said, the Greek god of wind.

"Keep your eye on the road, poltroon!" my father shouted affectionately. He didn't want to die yet. No low bridges, please—life was much too rich!

Every so often, just for fun, my grandfather would pull up at a country bus-stop and let a passenger—usually some stereotypical farmer's wife—board. The headscarfed woman, a basket of eggs under her arm, would see the appalling rite being enacted in the back seat and leave hurriedly, clucking. At this, both men would cackle uproariously.

During his Aeolian game, my father began to notice that his penis seemed to extend a little further each time he swung it. Perhaps this was due to the exciting conditions aboard the bus; all the windows were open, and so much wind rushed through the long, bright space that one would swear Aeolus was there in person, fanning the flames, puffing out his cheeks, and laughing.

Emboldened by this discovery, my father swung his appendage between two headrests and began to squeeze it full of blood.

"Watch out for my Orlon upholstery!" cried my grandfather, with the cheerful indulgence which was his trademark. Pre-ejaculate secretions or no, life was too short for scoldings!

My father ignored him, and kept squeezing. Soon his penis had extended between the headrests of the next row, and the next. Before long it lay the full length of the bus, its tip saluting my grandfather.

Seeing the opportunity for some fun, my grandfather pulled the bus over at the next stop. A young girl dressed in riding breeches climbed aboard, saw the red-faced beast blocking her path, screamed and ran away. My grandfather and father laughed until they wept.

"My liberty ends where the liberty of others begins," a wise man once said. It is a lesson that my father and grandfather seem never to have learned.

14

The Molester leaned back in the governor's swivel chair, making a church-and-steeple shape with his clasped hands. Behind him a bumble-bee beat against the glass of the window. The Murderer was lying sprawled across the governor's empty desktop.

"Are you sure we won't get caught in here?" I asked.

"Quite sure. The governor and all the admin staff are out buying prizes for the hobby sweepstakes. We have at least an hour," said the Molester.

"All right," said the Murderer, swinging into a sitting position, "meeting open. The purpose of this meeting is the baring of breasts. Clean breasts."

"I'd rather show a clean pair of heels," I said.

"We'll come to that presently. By the way, Sebastian, we're still in with you on that. But let's go back to the bare breasts. Over to you, Scotty."

"My name isn't Scotty," said the Molester. "Right, yes, as my friend the Murderer said, bare clean breasts. You admitted you were innocent. So are we. We both did nothing, in some cases repeatedly. I did nothing until someone died of it, the Molester did nothing to a child. I was accused of my nothing, he was accused of his. In both cases the filth had DNA traces proving that both he and I were the only ones who'd done the particular nothings we were accused of doing, or not doing, as the case may be. That's why we're here."

"We did nothing," repeated the Murderer. "But we like your idea that we should break out of here and do something—in fact, do the very things we were accused of, the things that led us here in the first place. By re-doing as something the nothing we didn't do first time around, we'll retrospectively vindicate the whole unjust process which got us banged up here. We'll reintroduce justice to the world, set wrongs to rights. You've appealed to our ethical side."

"And what's more," added the Molester, "doing the things we're accused of doing ought to be a right good larf."

"I'll have a good old murder," said the Murderer. "I swear it by murder!"

"And I'll have a good old molest," said the Molester. "I swear it by molestation!"

The two men performed a high five.

"What will you do?" they asked, turning to me. "What do you believe in? What will you swear by? Tell us your story."

"It was a snowy night in late June," I began, "and milk was spilling from the broken world's murdered head."

15

In my earliest memories, my parents are Heian.

By that I mean to say that, although we lived on a farm, my parents dressed very carefully. They had a strict and precise aesthetic code. They were like the aristocrats of Japan's Heian period, described by the Reverend James Murdoch (writing in Scotland at the end of the nineteenth-century) as "an ever-pullulating brood of greedy, needy, frivolous dilettanti—as often as not foully licentious, utterly effeminate, incapable of any worthy achievement, but withal the polished exponents of high breeding and correct form."

In fact, my parents' resemblance to this strutting, feathered, inbred "brood" makes the tragedy of my father's subsequent affair with a barnyard fowl—and the consequent downfall of the family dynasty—all the less surprising; an inevitability, perhaps. For, like Heian Japan, our farmhouse in the forests of Scotland was "an intellectual Sodom" full of "pampered minions and bepowdered poetasters."

Nevertheless, I am flooded with nostalgia—that most sensuously effulgent and effeminate of emotions—when I remember a typical scene on the farm. Dusk is falling, and the sky is seared with gashes of hot pink satin. Migrating geese are flying far overhead, for it is late summer. There is a cool breeze, scented with pine cones, drifting in from the dark, silent forest that surrounds our estate. On the raised wooden walkways leading from building to building—the "petal paths," we call them—ancient braziers have been lit. My mother sweeps by, followed at a discreet distance by two attendants who bear her train.

My mother lives in an elegant pavilion at the other end of the orchard. It is the custom for married people to live apart; this way they retain their dignity and independence. Joan spends much of her time writing in her pillowbook, or receiving admirers who court her with compact, elegant poems. It takes her so long to get dressed—even with several attendants helping—that she often spends six or seven hours preparing for a public appearance which will last only twenty minutes, and consist of a few highly formalized ritual gestures. You can see why, in these circumstances, she lives for her suitors, and the flutter these dandy supplicants bring to her heart.

My father, meanwhile, spends his time making highly detailed technical drawings with a mechanical pencil. The drawings depict utopian improvements he intends to make to the estate. We all know he will never implement these plans, and soon he admits it himself, turning his attention to his feathered friend instead.

It is at this moment that he bursts into my mother's summerhouse at the end of the orchard (wearing a particularly gorgeous and expensive kimono of which the dominant tones

are muted mossy greys, and the motif a pattern of pinus japon-
ica, the Japanese pine) and declares, "This is the pig I've been
fucking!"

It might seem like an impossibly vulgar gesture in such a
refined environment. And yet this too could be an expression
of refinement, an outburst on the part of a man for whom human sexual contact has become unbearably crude.

For Heians, nothing is more ugly than the naked human
body. Women wear five or six layers of robes, and make love
with them on. The sleeves are crucial; each garment has a
slightly different length and colour of material, and the sleeves
end, as a result, in exquisitely layered spectral and textural
ranges. But, for a man as highly sensitive and refined as my
father, it is likely that even the knowledge that his wife's robes
could be removed—whether they ever were or not—would
have been a torture. Enough, perhaps, to lead him to acts of
understandable adultery with a creature whose "clothes" were
physically attached to her, and who could only become "naked" when plucked as a preface to being cooked for lunch.

In comparison to this miraculous bird, then, any human
would naturally seem like a kind of pig. Yes, I can understand
my father.

You may think I am struggling unnecessarily hard to defend
him. Wasn't he, after all, being—technically—bestial when he
declared (to a goose, no less!) that his wife was "the pig I've been
fucking"? Why claim, in retrospect, that he was in fact a man of
exquisite sensibility, rarefied taste and unusual refinement? Why
should we—why should I, especially—not condemn him?

I will tell you why.

I must begin with the Hindu concept of dharma. Dharma is universal law, the law that sustains the universe.

Now, for some time—since I met the scary clown on top of the hill, and discovered that he was mere cardboard, and could be defeated with a small push—I have realized that my family history is governed, not by dharma, but by jokes.

Call it "joke dharma," if you like. Bad jokes, dirty jokes are, to my world, what the force of gravity is to yours. They shape every event in my life, and in the life of my family. I am not sure why it is so, but that it is, I cannot doubt. As a result, I live in a grim mirror world. I am a character trapped in a book of jokes—jokes, furthermore, which are in very poor taste.

I have discovered that there is a way to escape this grim fate—the misfortune of joke dharma. The solution, I believe, is that I should assume, myself, the responsibility of telling the very jokes which constrain and define me, and to make, each time, a small alteration in their telling, an alteration which restores a few shreds of dignity, human decency, beauty and sensuality to the tale.

It might begin by embroidery; I add a few details which are not normally included in the rush to the punchline. I must ensure that the story is so well-told that my audience loses interest in the farcical pay-off, the money-shot. I tell the tale several times, from different angles and with different emphases, forcing my listeners to pay attention to small formal questions, adverbs rather than verbs, hows rather than whats.

By these methods, little by little, I believe I can improve my world. Even if you are not in the same grim situation as me, you might want to try this technique yourself.

My mother called me to her summerhouse at the end of the orchard and asked me if I was happy. I answered with admirable concreteness: I would be happy if I had an ice cream.

Resplendent in fourteen layers of robes, sitting diagonally at her table with an earthenware cup of powdery green tea in front of her, my mother frowned.

"Ice cream will spoil your appetite," she said. "Go outside and compose poetry in the orchard. Bring me a tanka in half an hour."

The tanka is a five-line poem with alternating lines of five and seven syllables. It must concern nature, the seasons, love or other strong emotions. In the formulaic compactness of its shape it resembles a joke, but in spirit it is something else entirely, something far-away and lovely; sun catching mountains, rivers with rushing water, cold white snow on rocks, tree branches glazed with white frost, white sparkling snow in the world.

But the more I thought of mountains and sparkling snow, the more I thought of the ice cream I wanted to eat. Happiness for a seven-year-old is a very specific thing.

"Mother, I don't want to compose a tanka. I want to eat ice cream!"

"All right, just play in the orchard."

"But there's no one there! I don't want to play alone! The wind is chilly. There are ghosts in the orchard! I want to stay here with you!"

My mother smiled, recognizing immediately that I had replied within the formal restraints of a tanka.

"Very well," she said, "you can stay here with me and play. What shall we play at?"

"Let's play mummies and daddies," I said.

My mother looked a little surprised, but went along with it.

"All right, we'll do that. What do you want me to do?"

"Go to your sleeping quarters and lie down on the futon. I shall arrive presently." I was already assuming my father's tone of voice.

While my mother undressed, I pulled on a robe my father had left hanging in the cupboard. Adopting his loose-limbed gait (though somewhat impeded by the too-long robe), I clumped slowly towards the bedroom, gripping between my teeth the "Konig Suitor"-brand pipe he had left smouldering on the high mantelpiece during his last visit. Strangely, it was still lit.

When I flung open the screen door my mother raised herself on one elbow. She was completely naked, her legs welcomingly parted.

"What shall I do now?" she asked.

I closed the sliding door and adopted the gruff voice of my father:

"Give your son a big plate of ice cream, you cow!"

No sooner had I spoken than the door behind me was flung open again. In stepped my father, with a goose under his arm.

"This is the pig I've been fucking," he said.

16

It was a snowy night in late June and milk was spilling from the broken world's murdered head. The dark smoke of a bonfire smeared the air like grey blood seeping from a bandage. Mr Archibald Absalom Wellington appeared before me, dressed in the robes of a courtly gamekeeper. Mr Deodatus Village beat a brittle clay drum and Miss Adelaide Bobo shuffled through a series of curtsies.

"The ballad of Sebastian Skeleton!" cried Mr Edgar Alas Newport News.

There was a rushing of muslin and the floor was smeared with resin. Mrs Augusta Snow, Mrs Felicity Trollop Pardon and Miss Diop-Stephanie Virtue Secret-rose Diop walked in a line behind me, their movements perfectly synchronized to mine. The cold green light shone brightly from behind our shoulders like a cloud of spores, casting red shadows on the boards in front of us.

"So we have killed this white woman," I said.

"So we have killed this white woman," echoed Mrs Augusta Snow, Mrs Felicity Trollop Pardon and Miss Diop-Stephanie Virtue Secret-rose Diop.

"So we have made an offering to the god of thunder!" I cried, and the thundersheet rattled in the wings.

"So we have made an offering to the god of thunder!" echoed Mrs Augusta Snow, Mrs Felicity Trollop Pardon and Miss Diop-Stephanie Virtue Secret-rose Diop.

"So we have made an offering to the god of lightning!" I cried, and the powder flashed in its crucible.

"So we have made an offering to the god of lightning!" repeated Mrs Augusta Snow, Mrs Felicity Trollop Pardon and Miss Diop-Stephanie Virtue Secret-rose Diop.

The cook stirred the pot, the sewing maid stitched at her hoop, the medical student laid out fibulae, the curate prayed.

I broke an egg of the grey and yellow lapwing on the breast of the dead white woman. The air was momentarily filled with the cries of guillemots.

"So let the black butterfly descend," I cried, and the black cloth representing the butterfly was thrown from high up in the rafters and beams.

"So let the black butterfly descend," repeated Mrs Augusta Snow, Mrs Felicity Trollop Pardon and Miss Diop-Stephanie Virtue Secret-rose Diop.

"I took off my clothes and we were naked together," I said.

"He took off his clothes and they were naked together," repeated the chorus.

"There under the blankets we could have been any size, big or small!"

"There under the blankets they could have been any size, big or small."

"In my hand I held a hen's egg, a normal hen's egg."

"In his hand he held a hen's egg, a normal hen's egg."

"With the other, like a blind man, I feel for your tummy."

"With the other, like a blind man, he feels for her tummy."

"I squeeze the egg harder and harder until it cracks."

"He squeezes the egg harder and harder until it cracks."

"The liquid spills across your tummy, the yellow and the clear."

"The liquid spills across her tummy, the yellow and the clear."

"I throw away the shell and feel with my hand where the liquid egg is splattered, oozing slowly."

"He throws away the shell and feels with his hand where the liquid egg is splattered," intone Mrs Snow, Mrs Trollop Pardon and Miss Diop-Stephanie Diop.

"With both hands I smear it in a widening circle across your warm skin."

"With both hands he smears it in a widening circle across her warm skin," repeats the chorus.

"When it's spread out in a big thin wet circle, I wait for the egg to dry."

"When it's spread out in a big thin wet circle, he waits for the egg to dry."

"Your breast skin feels crispy; the tiniest movement you make could cause the flakes to crackle and break up."

"Her breast skin feels crispy; the tiniest movement she makes could cause the flakes to crackle and break up."

"While the egg is drying on your tummy, I move to your ear and begin to whisper."

"While the egg is drying," Mrs Snow, Mrs Trollop Pardon and Miss Diop-Stephanie Diop repeat, "he moves to her ear and begins to whisper."

"Scratching the crispy egg skin, I begin to tell you a story."

And the women repeat the line, then fall silent and step back.

The lighting changes. Around the stage, amethyst begins to glint. The scent of eucalyptus curls through the theatre.

There is an ocean liner sailing across your tongue. The liner is huge, but your mouth is even bigger. Suddenly it runs into trouble—perhaps it has been punctured by one of your teeth—and begins to sink. All the hundreds of people inside the liner jump into the sea. On the surface of the sea—the surface of your tongue—they cling to whatever wreckage they can find. But just at that moment you swallow a gulp of fruit juice, and all the people are swept away, down your throat, to live in your tummy. They are inside your tummy, and the dried egg is outside it, with my hand moving in the darkness, gently loosening the dried flakes from your warm skin, your tiny fine skin hairs.

I am small now, and I am taking an extremely long journey, a polar exploration, to your feet. It feels far, far away from civilisation here. When I get to my destination, I grip your ankle with both hands and begin to lick the underside of your toes, wettening them, and lick into the spaces between the toes, until it feels cool and wet in there. I do it for a long time, and it makes me very, very happy.

"This is the taste and texture and temperature of my daughter's toes," I think, as I lick slowly, with enormous love.

Although it's dark down there, the exact shape of my daughter's toes emerges in my mind, a clear picture. I am "licking to see."

"I can see the sky!" shouts the Murderer. We hack a little more and the top of the tunnel falls in. It is indeed the sky. Cautiously, we emerge, all three of us, onto a suburban residential street. I can see the glass house just beyond the corner, partly obscured by trees.

17

Dad would only have dental work done in Bad Gastein, in the Salzkammergut municipality of the Austrian Alps. He liked to combine his check-ups with visits to the December Krampus celebrations—sinister pagan rituals in which unruly men with shaggy hair and goat horns ran riot through the village brandishing whips and sacks, sounding cowbells, and dragging chains behind them.

My father found a level of dental competence in Bad Gastein that he had never encountered elsewhere; laser drills, rich and smooth anaesthetics and fine prosthetic detailing.

He liked the contrast between Dr Schlammpeter's sterile, organised dental clinic and the pandemonium reigning outside. Often he would stagger out of the clinic, still groggy from dental drugs, only to be confronted by Klaubauf, the demonic assistant to Krampus. Wearing a shaggy yeti-skin and baring long fangs, the hideous open-nostrilled creature would proceed to whip my father's penis with a heavy chain.

"Yes, continue, fiend, do your worst!" my father would scream, "I can't feel a thing!"

One December, though, my father failed to have the usual luxurious anaesthetic. My sister Luisa took him to the surgery and, maliciously, announced that she wanted a tooth pulled. "Just pull it out as quick as you can, no anaesthetic, then we'll be off," she said.

"It's actually more expensive that way," said Dr Schlammpeter. "With pain it's €200, without pain only €100."

"Oh, we definitely want it with pain," said Luisa. "Father has to do a bit of after-dinner speaking at the hotel later, so we need him to stay sharp."

"Which tooth do you want pulled?" asked the dentist.

"This one here." Luisa indicated a lupine side incisor in my father's mouth.

"You know," said my father nervously, "if it's cheaper without pain, let's do it without."

"I'll tell you what," said Dr Schlammpeter, "I'm going to give you some Viagra first."

My father looked surprised. "Will that kill the pain?"

"Not really," said Schlammpeter. "But it'll give you something to hold onto while I work on the tooth."

My father swallowed the tablet then grabbed the dentist's penis through his trousers.

"What are you doing?" demanded Schlammpeter.

"You aren't going to hurt me, are you?" asked my father. It was, under the circumstances, a rhetorical question.

"Anything else you want to ask me before we begin?" said Schlammpeter, enjoying the pressure of my father's hand around his penis.

"Yes," said my father, "will I be able to play the trumpet after this operation?"

"Certainly," said Schlammpeter.

"That's wonderful, because I can't play it now," said my father.

Schlammpeter smiled grimly—he'd heard it before—and strapped my father into the chair, which faced towards the surgery window. The operation began, accompanied by the sickening silence of laser drills.

Suddenly my father caught sight of the horrific face of Klaubauf framed in the open window. He began shouting, but the dentist couldn't see the monster and thought my father was simply screaming in pain.

"Hey," warned Schlammpeter, "I told you, with pain this will cost you twice as much!"

When the operation was over Schlammpeter unstrapped my father and detached the dental brace from his mouth. The two men released hold of each other's penises. Luisa came over.

"Have your teeth stopped hurting yet?" she asked.

"I don't know," lisped Dad, indistinctly. "Schlammpeter has them."

"I'm so pissed off with Dad," Luisa told me as we sat side by side in an abandoned sleigh, overlooking the snowy track that led down to the village.

"Why?"

"Because he broke my doll, Hanna, the one I lost."

"He had Hanna all that time?"

"He must've been keeping her for some strange reason. And then he brought her back broken!"

"Did he tell you how it happened?"

"That's the worst thing," said Luisa. "He told me he'd never borrowed Hanna in the first place, and that when he'd given her back to me Hanna hadn't been broken. Then he added that Hanna had already been broken when he'd first borrowed her, and that a broken doll is in fact more charming than an unbroken one, and that therefore it was a real shame Hanna wasn't in fact broken . . ."

"But *she* was broken!"

"Yes, she was broken all right. Then he told me that, in a sense, every broken doll is whole and every unbroken doll is in fragments."

"He's a nutter!"

"He followed that with the information that Hanna both was and was not broken, depending on how you looked at it. Then he said that, although the doll was mine, her brokenness was his, and that he had broken Hanna for her own good. Then Dad started to cry and said that nothing could replace my broken Hanna, so 'Here's nothing!' And he made as if to hand me nothing."

"Honestly! The fuckface!"

"He wasn't finished, either. He told me—quite seriously—that what's important now is not the unbroken doll, but how she has broken our hearts, therefore making us whole and joining us together. 'We have all been broken by this non-doll Hanna,' he said, 'who has therefore healed us.' I was weeping too by this point. He's a clever old bastard, Dad."

"He is, too."

Just at that moment Dad stepped out of the dentist's office. He was immediately confronted by Klaubauf. Taller than ever this year, the shaggy monster had goat bells mounted on his horns, two whips, a chain, and horn-rimmed spectacles framing his fierce, piercing eyes. In daily life he was Schlumm the librarian.

"You need some dental treatment urgently," joked Sebastian. "Either that, or start wearing a yellow tie to match your teeth."

Klaubauf, unamused, set about whipping the phallus dragging along behind my father. The organ was strapped to a small sleigh.

"Stop, that stings!" protested Sebastian. Not only was there no anaesthetic this year to dull the pain, but the Viagra had given Klaubauf a bigger target.

"This dentist has a reputation as painless," said Klaubauf, "but he isn't painless at all. When I whip him he screams just like everybody else."

"That's funny," said Sebastian. "By the way, why did you appear in the window and frighten me halfway through my operation?"

"Oh, Dentist Schlammpeter asked me to do that," said Schlumm. "He knew your screams would clear his waiting room. He has some important work to do this afternoon."

It was only when my father reached the hotel where he was to deliver his speech that it really hit home: not a single tooth remained in his head.

The guests were assembled and the master of ceremonies was already clinking a glass to hush the crowd. Sebastian turned in desperation to the two men sitting next to him. "I have no teeth," he lisped.

"That's no problem," chorused the two hooded figures. They were Bim and Spot, the beekeepers from my uncle's funeral. "We have some extras."

The beekeepers rummaged about in a briefcase they seemed to share and produced a set of false teeth. They were mechanical joke teeth that clacked together when you wound up a little red knob. My father tried to fit them into his head, but they were useless.

"Wait," said Bim, "try these." He reached into the briefcase and produced another pair. This time they looked more realistic. My father tried them on. The MC was just announcing his speech.

"Better," he whispered, "but they're a bit loose. People will think I have a severe speech impediment."

"I have one more pair," said Spot. The lights were being dimmed and my father was rising to speak. He slipped the final set of dentures in behind a napkin. This time, luckily, they fitted perfectly.

My father's speech was a resounding success. His dentures held out until the end. After he'd accepted the ovation with a gracious bow, my father turned to Bim and Spot.

"Are you here for the Krampus run?" he asked.

"Yes," the keepers chorused, "we come every year."

"Splendid," said my father. "And thank you so much for the dentures. Do you want them back?"

"Oh, you can keep them," said Bim and Spot. "We've been paying for our trip by helping out at the local funeral home. Plenty more where those came from."

18

After we'd escaped, just before we went to commit the crimes that we'd been falsely accused of, the Murderer, the Molester and I spent a few hours birdwatching at Inner Forest.

Inner Forest was the wood next to the glass house. I knew that it contained a family of Greater Crested Grebes. I knew this because in prison I had subscribed to a birdwatching newsletter which reported that hatchlings had been spotted riding on their mother's back as she scrabbled across the gravel pit in the forest clearing. This was a notable event indeed; Greater Crested Grebes hadn't been seen at Inner Forest in over a century.

A pathological Grebe-killing individual had executed the last known local community of the fowl in 1889. What's worse, he had done it whilst they were in their breeding plumage. He had used his bare hands. The few remaining individuals, traumatized by the ordeal of watching the event, had taken wing.

We were pushing our way through tough, spiky pine branches as I told the men this. The Murderer and the Molester shook their heads.

"How could a human being hurt a flock of innocent birds like that?" demanded the Molester.

"Because humans are scum, that's why," said the Murderer. "They should all be hacked to the ground with a blunt machete and left to rot, swarming with flies. Filthy scum."

"I dunno," said the Molester, "birds can be disappointing too."

"Why?" asked the Murderer.

"Corruption," said the Molester. "They line their nests, if you know what I mean."

"No, I don't know what you mean. Of course they line their nests. That's natural."

"They line them with feathers, straw, paper clips, scraps of blanket, pompoms, jewelry, insulation wire, pornography, shoe-laces in all colours, Scotch tape, kid gloves, banknotes . . ."

"What are you trying to say?"

"They're common criminals, birds, no better than you or me. That's all I'm saying. They should all be locked up."

"Well, they are locked up," said the Murderer. "Half the birds you see are in cages."

"That's what I mean," said the Molester.

"Listen, you two!" I said, holding my hand up to my lips.

Through the dark forest glades rang the unmistakable, mournful cry of the Grebe.

"Lovely, isn't it?"

"No," said the Murderer, "it's 'orrible. It sounds like some-one getting strangled. In fact, I wouldn't be surprised if that's what it was."

"Maybe Grebes are like parrots," said the Molester. "They repeat what they hear. Maybe this bird's ancestor witnessed an 'orrible murder, recorded the sounds, and passed them on to its descendents, which have been playing them back ever since. Like a broken tape recorder."

"Shut up," I said, "it's you that's the broken tape recorder! Why can't you just enjoy the sounds of nature? The wind in the trees, the sound of a river in the distance, the call of birds, beasts and insects? It's idyllic!"

"I'm just saying . . ." said the Murderer. "Nature red in tooth and claw and all that. We shouldn't project our own desires onto it. Anthropopopomorphism, that is."

"Anthropopopowhat?" said the Molester.

"Anthropopopomorphism," said the Murderer. "It means when you see animals as little people, walking around on all fours. Or when you see birds as feathery little people with beady eyes and beaks."

"That's stupid, nobody sees birds as feathery little people with beady eyes," said the Molester.

"Some do," said the Murderer. "Sickos. That's why there are so many cases of bestiality. You know, people caught with their trousers around their ankles, fucking a bird."

"When was the last person caught with his trousers down fucking a bird?" said the Molester.

"I don't know, I don't read the avian press," said the Murderer. "But I'm sure it happens all the time."

There was a moment of silence. Then the Molester spoke.

"Where does a 226.796185 kilogram Greater Crested Grebe sit?" he asked.

"I don't know," said the Murderer. "Where does a 226.796185 kilogram Greater Crested Grebe sit?"

There was a pause.

"If you two don't shut up we're going to have to abandon this birdwatching expedition," I snapped, "and just go and commit our crimes."

"Why don't we do that, Prof?" said the Murderer. "The Molester and I are getting cold hands anyway. This was a stupid idea. We're not equipped. We don't have binoculars, sitting sticks or thermos flasks of tea. We don't even have guns in case 226-kilogram Grebes attack."

"Yeah," agreed the Molester. "We're murderers and molesters. We're not cut out to be birdwatchers. This is too hard on sensitive men like us."

"All right," I sighed, "let's go and commit our crimes. I suppose we'll have all the time in the world to go birdwatching after."

"I hear there are pigeons at the Scrubs," said the Murderer.

19

Nao, the Japanese lodger, fed Luisa and me at seven o'clock sharp each evening, spreading the kitchen table with a crowd of differently-sized, differently-painted dishes featuring fishes, swirls, boats, checker patterns, leaf motifs. Each one contained a few morsels of peculiar but delicious food. "Whale knuckle," she'd explain. Or "preservation fish." Or "sweet red bean."

Her duties done, Nao would retreat to her room upstairs. She mostly liked to spend her time alone, drawing, with the floor-length window open and the sound of rain at dusk pattering on the leaves of the wood.

Nao's room, lit harshly by a round overhead fluorescent light, smelled sweetly of tatami. She had little furniture; her whole life was centred on the matted floor. On the low table where she sat most of the time, coloured pens and pencils crowded a compartmentalized clear plastic box which looked like a tiny model of the glass house itself.

When Nao needed sleep, she unrolled a horsehair sleeping mat, threw it across the length of the small room, and threw herself down on it. Above her window a fitted air-conditioner whooshed soothingly; her filtered, cooled air was the best in the house.

The glass walls of Nao's room were scattered with tacked-up drawings she'd been working on. They were simple, organic, stringy, hand-coloured, splashy, crude and subtle. The more she drew, the more she Blu-Tacked up, the more privacy she had.

Unfortunately, Dad didn't respect Nao's privacy at all.

"You know," he said, sliding open her door and stepping naked onto her tatami-mat floor from the adjacent bathroom, "I get so sweaty in the bath that I have to take a shower right afterwards!"

Nao was polite but distant. She had a habit of thinking the best of people until the very last possible moment.

"Thank you for thinking of me to tell this fact to," she said, turning discreetly to the window and pretending to relight the insect-repelling incense coil. She could still see my father in the reflection on the glass wall. His dangling cock hung like an elephant's trunk, dripping onto her tatami like an over-inked calligraphy brush.

"Ah," exclaimed Nao, "accidentally there is a water dripping. Let me help you."

She ran over, tore off a wad of kitchen towel, and began to mop up the puddle forming around the tip of dad's penis.

Suddenly my father let rip an enormous fart. It smelled of sulphur and hung in the centre of the room like a curly brown cloud.

"That is very interesting," said Nao, as if he had merely made an instructive remark. "I think the same thing sometimes."

"Ah," said Dad, "thinking aloud again, sorry."

He knelt closer to the kotatsu table. There were a couple of drawings on tracing paper, and a map of the settlements of forgotten Siberian tribes living around the Sea of Okhotsk: Nao had been studying the disappearing culture of the Evenki and Eveny peoples; the Negidals, Oroks and Koryaks.

"Lovely earthenware flute you have here," said Dad, fingering the paperweight that held these various papers down.

"This is called iwabue," said Nao. "It is Japanese stone flute. It has been in my family for many generations. Would you like to hear its music?"

"Certainly," said Sebastian. He picked up the flute and was about to fix it to the lips of his anus when Nao snatched it away.

"No, first I shall play," she corrected.

Obediently, my father tucked his penis under him like a cushion.

Nao raised the instrument to her lips and the room was filled with a haunting sound, a concert of ancient, coloured human breath which threw my father into a trance. He sagged towards the floor, and soon fell fast asleep.

Drawn by the music and the sound of my father's snores, Luisa and I edged around the sliding door, saw Dad's heaped naked flesh, and began to tug his unresisting body across the tatami, towards his own bedroom. As we dragged him over the threshold we turned and bowed to Nao. She returned our bow with a nod and a smile, but didn't stop playing. The moment she stopped, Father would wake up.

20

The Murderer, the Molester and I snapped the last few spiny branches, clambered over the fence and exited the Inner Forest. It was a relief to be back on tarmacadam.

The lights of the glass house were visible just around the next corner. Silhouettes of adults and children could be seen milling around inside. Who were they—Peter, Luisa, Sebastian, Nao, Billy Plantagenet, Joan? Or somebody else entirely?

"What time is it?" asked the Molester, gazing at those mysterious shapes with some anxiety.

I looked at my watch. "11:30."

"And we're going to commit our crimes today, aren't we?"

"Yes. You're not backing out now, are you?"

"No, no, of course not. But we'll be arrested pretty soon after, and sent back to prison, won't we?"

"Of course. But we'll have the satisfaction of our crimes this time—those atrocious, delirious crimes we've dreamed of, and sworn by, for so long!—and also the satisfaction of knowing that we aren't wrongfully imprisoned. It's going to be great, lads! Our whole lives will fall into place! For the first time, everything will make sense."

"Oh, I don't doubt that, Professor. Not for a moment. It's just that . . . well, my crime is the kind of thing best committed at night."

"Mine too," said the Murderer. "It's a night crime."

I could see the men were nervous. These weren't hardened criminals; they were pure, green, soft. Deep in their pockets, their hands trembled.

"All right," I said, "we'll commit our crimes when darkness falls. That gives us, what, six or seven hours. What shall we do?"

The Murderer and the Molester thought for a while.

"Let's go to a picture gallery," said the Molester. "I've always liked pictures."

"Yes," said the Murderer. "Paintings, nice restful old ones. With people in."

The Municipal Museum had a surprisingly good collection of Renaissance altarpieces, screens, and religious allegories, with a sprinkling of lesser-known names from the Flemish School, some Davids, and even a minor Goya of dubious pedigree. What's more, it was free to get in, and the café wasn't bad at all. Better than the prison canteen, anyway.

The Murderer, the Molester and I had the place pretty much to ourselves. True, a party of schoolgirls shared the building, but they were herded efficiently into the dimly-lit musical instruments room, where they sat cross-legged on the floor, sketching and showing their panties to the guards.

To avoid inflaming the ex-convicts' carnal lust—it was a long time since they had seen human panties—I steered them towards David's *Intervention of the Sabine Women*.

The two men stood before the magnificent canvas for several minutes, feasting with their eyes on the naked buttocks of the soldiers, the bare-breasted women imploring on their knees, the cherubs spread out on the ground like so much sushi, the rampant sea of spears.

The Murderer broke the silence.

"A lot of murder going on there," he nodded, knowingly.

"No," said the Molester with a wink. "Rape."

"You're both wrong," I said. My long hours in the Art History aisles of the prison library hadn't been in vain. "I'll tell you what's actually going on."

I stood in front of the painting, positioning myself so that I could point out specific figures on the battlefield.

"On the left here you see the ramparts of Rome. When Romulus founded it, Rome was a city of men. There were no women at all."

"Sounds familiar," murmured the Molester.

A couple of straggler schoolgirls had drifted in from the music room and hunkered down against the far wall to listen, inadvertently giving me views of their panties.

"Realising that their race couldn't survive without women," I continued, "the Romans organised a festival dedicated to Neptune, god of the sea. They invited their neighbours the Sabines and, at a signal from Romulus, suddenly seized the Sabine women and carried them away to Rome, fighting off the pursuing Sabine men, who were mostly the womens' fathers."

"They must've picked young ones," said the Molester to one of the schoolgirls.

"Once they got to Rome, Romulus convinced the women to marry Romans—to exchange Sabine fathers for Roman husbands. And to sweeten the deal he gave them property and civil rights much better than anything they'd have had back in the Sabine world. Most of the women accepted, and soon enough started having babies by their new husbands, the Romans."

"Are there any paintings of the fucking, Prof?" demanded the Murderer.

The schoolgirls thought this was hilarious and convulsed in giggles.

"No," I said. "There are no paintings of the fucking. But a year or so later the women's dads put together a Sabine Dad's Army and marched on Rome. They were determined to get their daughters back."

I waved my arms at the naked battle scene.

"Look at it," I cried. "Freud would have loved this! Phallic spears at forty-five degrees! An army of fathers versus an army of husbands! Two generations at war! And in between them, the women, with their babies at their feet, trying to stop their husbands and their fathers from tearing each other—and them!—to pieces! Look at this one, holding her baby up in the air! It's as if she's saying to the Sabines 'Look, if you attack the Romans you attack your own sons-in-law, the fathers of your grandchildren!' And, simultaneously, saying to the Romans 'Look, if you attack the Sabines you're killing your fathers-in-law!'"

"Did it work?" said the Molester, looking as if he hoped it all ended in carnage.

"It did indeed. The men admitted their ties of blood and made a truce. They downed their weapons and, from that moment on, lived together in harmony."

The family theme was obviously getting through to the audience. The schoolgirls chewed gum, the white-socked balls of their heels tucked tightly into the warm, deep nook of their panties. The Molester looked suddenly as if he were about to cry.

"Were any of the Sabines and the Romans each other's uncles?" asked the Murderer.

21

My family never celebrated birthdays. I woke up on the morning of my birthday with a heavy feeling in my chest. Who would remember and, even if they remembered, who would care?

I walked naked into my father's bedroom. The beast was snoring.

"Guess how old I am today!" I demanded.

My father spluttered, tossed, and woke up.

"What?" he growled.

"Guess how old I am today!"

"I have no idea," said my father. Then he turned over.

"I'm eleven," I shouted. But he was already asleep.

I pulled on some clothes and walked down the glass staircase to the kitchen.

My grandfather happened to be visiting us that day, mere months before someone would tell the joke which would kill him in his sleep.

"Guess how old I am today, Grandpa!" I said.

"Let me guess," said Grandpa. "Come here!"

He stuck his hand down my trousers and played with my testicles. It went on for an hour. He squeezed them, kneaded them, rolled them around, fished for them, caught them, then threw them back.

He cooked my testicles in an omelette, ate them, complimented the chef, threw up, demanded to see the manager, had a violent altercation with the man, plunged a knife into his belly, handed the resultant meat to the chef, asked for it to be lightly sautéed and served on a bed of thinly-sliced zucchini with its own blood for gravy, and served the dish to the ghost of his wife, my grandmother, the village whore.

Out of the corner of my eye, while all this was going on, I seemed to see Balthus painting us, holding up his brush from behind an easel in the corner of the room.

"Are you really in love with young girls?" I asked Balthus, like a child.

Balthus wrinkled his brow and turned to me. Outside, the mountains of Switzerland shimmered in an early summer haze.

"I am interested in form, nothing more. Form in its youth, and the form of youths."

Finally my grandfather took his hand out of my trousers and said, "You're eleven years old."

"How did you know?" I asked.

"I heard you tell your father."

22

At dusk the Murderer, the Molester and I would commit the crimes of which we had been so falsely accused. It would be the perfect revenge for the miscarriage of justice that had put us in prison.

In the meantime, the Murderer, the Molester and I still had time to kill. We decided to catch a train at random and see where it took us.

We made our way to the station. It was a fine day for an expedition; small, ragged clouds sped across the sky and the undersides of fresh leaves flashed white.

On the platform we bought three bento boxes—flatpack self-assembly lunches in the Japanese fashion, containing morsels of dried meat, fish and chicken, slices of pickled vegetable, string beans, small dollops of egg and potato salad, rice surmounted by a sour plum, and a sweet treat for after.

Our tickets were first class—this was the last train trip we would be making for some time, so we wanted to make the best of it. The carriage seemed completely empty—we had the best compartment to ourselves. We hung our three beige raincoats on pegs behind us, placed our lunch boxes on our knees, snapped open the simple wooden chopsticks supplied and tucked into the delicious food.

Directly on time the train pulled away from the platform, and soon the views of city chimneys were replaced by oak trees, cows and foxgloves. We were filled with a spirit of cheerful adventure, of freedom, of possibility. Conversation revolved around a variety of themes: childhood holidays, favourite sexual positions, maker's marks on Etruscan pottery, Jack the Ripper's alibis, numerology, palindromes, and the best way to mustard up a croque monsieur.

Suddenly the train slammed to a halt in a tunnel, and in the screeching of brakes was mixed another sound: a human scream.

"What the . . . !"

"I say!"

"This is rum!"

"Goodness gracious!"

The Murderer, the Molester and I sat in the dark for a few seconds. The Murderer pulled his brass cigarette lighter from his pocket and lit it. The Molester rose from his seat and tried the compartment door. No good; it wouldn't budge. I reached for the timepiece in my waistcoat pocket and read it by the light of the Murderer's flame. It was 1:25 P.M.

"Gentlemen," announced the Molester, "it seems the power supply to the door has failed. We are trapped in here and would do well, I think, to remain calm and wait for help to arrive."

"Well," said the Murderer, nodding at me, "it looks like your dad's been driving this train!"

"If he were," I returned, with a grim sparkle, "we should now be at the pearly gates instead of trapped in this tunnel."

"Quite so," returned the Murderer, "my remark was intended in jest."

Our ordeal was not long—as quickly as it had stopped, the train started again, and soon we were back in the sunshine and the green fields. At the next station, though, the train made an unscheduled stop. A party of policemen boarded our carriage, led by a moustached man in plain clothes. There were muffled voices through the compartment wall, then, presently a group of paramedics boarded the train and removed what appeared to be a body on a stretcher. For a moment we caught a glimpse of young naked limbs, bloodied and dangling.

Three gasps rang out. The Murderer, the Molester and I exchanged concerned glances.

There came a tap on the door.

"Come in?"

The detective tried to enter, but couldn't open the jammed door.

"It's blocked," we mimed through the glass. The detective tapped his watch and disappeared. Some minutes later he returned with railway staff equipped with drills, spanners and a blow-torch. By the application of metal and fire, the engineers succeeded in opening the door.

"Inspector Spectre," said the detective, extending a hand. "I wonder if you wouldn't mind answering a few questions?"

The Murderer, the Molester and I indicated the empty seat and bade Spectre to sit down. He removed his coat—identical to ours—hung it on the free peg and took his place in the seat, crossing his legs and filling a briarwood pipe with sweetly scented tobacco.

"There has been a death in the next compartment," he began, shaking out his match. "The naked body of a young girl of about twelve has been discovered, brutally murdered and sexually . . . interfered with. Her clothes were not discovered. Apart from you three gentlemen, the girl was the only passenger in this entire carriage. What's more, the technical staff tell me a power failure has kept every door firmly locked for the past hour. The murder occurred at exactly 1:25 P.M., when the train came to a halt in the tunnel."

"Could someone have entered the First Class carriage from Second Class?" drawled the Murderer. His accent and mannerisms had taken a surprising turn towards the aristocratic.

"Impossible, sir," replied the detective, puffing a cloud of aromatic pipe smoke towards the compartment ceiling. "The doors at either end were also blocked. Nobody could have entered or left this compartment."

"But by the same token," said the Molester, "we cannot be blamed. As the other gentlemen will vouch, we were also unable to open our door when the train stopped."

We confirmed that this had indeed been the case.

"That remains to be seen," replied the inspector, tapping the paneling of the compartment with his knuckles and tilting his head to capture every nuance of the resulting sound.

"Did you hear any suspicious sounds, or see anything when the train stopped in the tunnel?" he asked.

"As a matter of fact," I replied, "we did. There was, mixed in with the squealing train brakes, the sound of a human scream."

"Can you describe it?" asked the detective, reaching into his inside breast pocket for a small spiral-bound notepad.

"Well, it was . . . strangled," said the Murderer. "I've only heard screams like that when people are actually being strangled. There's a bit of a death rattle built in, plus a high-pitched cry, plus a gripped kind of note, like the sound of someone playing a cheap rubber clarinet while wearing a high-quality pair of welding gloves."

The detective scribbled this down and glanced suspiciously at the Murderer. "You seem to be quite an expert on the sound of strangling," he said. "How so?"

"Oh," said the Murderer, "I read a lot of detective fiction."

"I see," said Spectre. "Did you notice anything else suspicious? Any activity in the tunnel, for instance?"

"I saw . . . I saw a gentleman out there, making off," said the Molester.

"Making off in the tunnel?" said the inspector, sitting up a little and raising his pen.

"Yes, in the tunnel," said the Molester, looking at us.

"Did either of you see this person?" asked the inspector.

We shook our heads. "It was very dark in the tunnel," I said.

"Can you describe the gentleman?" said the inspector.

"He was . . . a dark gentleman," replied the Molester. "Coal black, of swarthy complexion."

"Do you mean a Negro?" asked the inspector.

"I couldn't see, it was dark," said the Molester, and added: "I would prefer not to use racial epithets."

"Yes," protested the Molester. "Racial epithets are not relevant to this case. Shame on you, Inspector!"

The inspector looked embarrassed and made a note in his book.

"I hope you gentlemen were not in a hurry to get anywhere," he said at last. "I may have to detain you for some while."

"We have no pressing appointments until dusk," I said. "We are at your disposal, Superintendent."

"I am actually not a Superintendent," said Spectre. "I am an amateur detective, subsidised by private means."

"The details of your income need not concern us," said the Murderer, even-handedly. "There is no need to be defensive."

"I should warn you, though, that I have solved many crimes."

"How is that a warning?" I asked. "The sooner you solve this crime, the sooner we can commit—the sooner we can go about our business, no?"

"I very much hope so," said the inspector. "I very much hope to get to the bottom of this nasty business before the police arrive."

"You mean those were not policemen who accompanied you aboard the train?"

"Actors," Spectre explained, blowing a Chinese dragon of opium smoke into the air above our heads. "And now, if you will excuse me, I must go and make a call of nature. I mean, visit the body of the victim, currently being stored in the Gentlemen's toilet."

Spectre rose, threw his coat over his arm, saluted us, clicked his heels, and left the compartment. After a few moments we saw him crossing the platform and entering the Gentlemen's convenience, from which a thin trickle of blood could clearly be seen emerging. Presently we saw the man's shifty eyes at the open window, and a trickle of yellow urine mingled with the blood in the gutter.

"Now would be the time to make a run for it," said the Molester, looking distinctly uneasy.

"Yes, let's break this window and strike out across country," said the Murderer.

Escape, however, was unnecessary. Before Spectre had time to close his flies the train began to pull away from the country station and was soon flying through verdant fields once more, for all the world as if nothing had happened.

"The police will make short work of that pervert's story," said the Molester.

"Yes," agreed the Murderer, "it looks as though the filthy swine's alibi has just puffed off."

Both men laughed heartily.

23

It was during a family holiday on Summerisle that I lost my virginity.

We returned to this Ionic-Hebridean pearl each year. The island was the ancestral seat of our family, and its single tree-less mountain resembled a craggy throne.

Since cars were unknown on the island, people travelled strapped to the fleecy bellies of sheep, which were enormous in those parts. The more adventurous rode goats, which tended to trot faster, climb higher, and strike out on their own more readily than their creamy cousins.

By this point my father had mellowed somewhat. Instead of making his offspring yield to incest, he concentrated on high-yielding offshore bank accounts, or fishing. He had a choice of fishing styles; he either sat on the crags above the sea, dangling a rod into the breakers below, or fished down his own trousers with his hand.

This trouser fishing—once his favourite hobby—my father had by now begun to find unsatisfactory. The game somewhat lacked in suspense, for the caught creature—although big!—was always the same, and furthermore was attached to his own body, which meant that when he caught it he was immediately obliged either to throw it back into its element alive, or else castrate himself.

Each year my father and I would make our way, within a day or so of arrival on Summerisle, to the wooden hut at the foot of the mountain. It was here that enterprising goatherds had set up a goat rental business. Visitors requiring instruction in goat-riding—and we were still novices!—could also hire, by the hour, the services of a qualified instructor.

On the year in question—the year I lost my virginity!—we made our way to the goat hut only to find a new receptionist, a very pretty young girl dressed in Orkney tweed. All the goatherds were out on the mountain, but the receptionist told us she could reserve a session for us. Did we have a favourite instructor?

My father did—the fellow from last year had been excellent, coaching Dad and me to intermediate goat-handling competency—but couldn't remember his name.

"Well," asked the receptionist, "can you remember what he looked like, or any particular distinguishing features he had?"

"Yes," said my father, "now you mention it I do remember something distinctive. He had two anuses."

The receptionist flushed tartan red. "Two anuses? What do you mean?" she stammered.

"Well," said my father, "I remember that as my son and I were returning to the shed, one of the other guides shouted out to our man: Hallo there! How's it going with those two arseholes of yours?"

It was shortly after this episode that my father and I began to bond in a way we never had before. His sexual quirks were subsiding. He had once been a monster, certainly, but at last, it seemed to me, he was learning to be human.

But—as is often the way with these things!—it is precisely when the criminal ceases his crimes and drops his guard that detection is most likely.

Word began to spread on Summerisle that a solitary Englishman sojourning on the island, Howard Kingsley by name, was not everything he at first appeared to be.

Our first encounter with Kingsley came at a point when my father was in the throes of recidivism. He had purchased a monk's robe, tied it at the waist with a length of rope and, wearing no underwear beneath it, was sprawling by a fountain on the village square, giving a gaggle of local children a clear view of his genitalia.

He was about to start fishing when Kingsley strode up. "Excuse me, gentlemen," he said, "but I wonder if you could help me. I'm compiling a study of sexual mores on the island, and trying to interview as many people as I can about their sexual practices."

My father tugged the hem of his robe back down below his knees.

"We may be able to assist," he said, warily. "This is my son. He's fourteen."

And I found the sexologist's spongelike hand in mine.

He explained that he was conducting government-funded research into sex, but neither of us believed a word of it. My father and I were both thinking the same thought: that this charlatan was in fact conducting government-funded research into sex. After conferring behind our hands, we decided to play along with this truth masquerading as the truth by telling him the truth masquerading as the truth.

And so I told Kingsley a long and unlikely-sounding story about my sexual awakening on the island. I began by describing how I spied from the water-reeds on the local girls as they bathed naked in the mountain stream, then continued with tales of casual bestiality as I flicked the highland cows' tails aside and availed myself of their warm innards, then moved onto blow jobs from the bequiffed grandmother who kept dubious lodgings on the village square. My own grandmother, in fact.

Kingsley remained silent and impassive as I told him these tales, which were all, by the way, true—it is with my own grandmother that I lost my virginity. He scribbled the accounts down in a notebook bound in elegant purple velum, then turned to my father. "And you, sir, what have you to tell me?"

"I would advise you not to believe a word of what my son has just said," my father began. "He has a rather vivid imagination. What's more, I recognized some of that nonsense from cheap jokes I've heard circulating."

"On the other hand, every word of what I will now tell you is true. I swear it on the memory of my mother, the town whore."

And my father gave a complete and truthful account of his entire sexual life, from beginning to end. Kingsley turned white, and then green, and then crimson, and then blue. At the twenty-minute mark he began to vomit. Then he cleaned up his own mess, uttered curses, said prayers, recited multiplication tables, and took up his pen again. At last my father finished with a charming tale from his youth.

He was courting Joan, who lived at the time on a nearby farm. One evening, as my father and Joan sat trouser fishing on the crags, he spotted a highland bull mounting a shaggy ginger cow. The animals began to hump, illuminated by the orange rays of the fucking sun.

It was the moment, my father decided, to make a pass at Joan. "I'd love to be doing what that bull is doing right now," he whispered.

"Well," replied Joan, "why don't you—it's your cow!"

"That is all completely untrue," I said. "Everything my father has just told you is a lie."

"Shall I tell you what happened when my grandmother found out my sister Luisa's dirty little secret?"

"All right," said Kingsley, warily. My father made to gag me, but Kingsley waved him off.

Luisa was selling herself. She had digs on the square, a squalid room alongside a lot of other rooms used by other girls on the game. She wasn't telling anyone in the family. Well, one day the police raided the brothel and arrested the lot of them. All the little whores.

They lined them up on the street outside. And who should be walking past at that moment but Grandma.

"Your grandmother?" asked Kingsley.

"No," said my father.

"Yes," I said.

"Continue," instructed the sexologist, making a note in the margins of the page.

Luisa was pulling gargoyle faces, desperately hoping Gran wouldn't recognize her. But Gran walked right up.

"Little Luisa, gurning like a gargoyle!" exclaimed Gran, with a hint of malice in her voice. "What are you queuing for?"

Luisa cast around for some convenient lie. "They're handing out soft-boiled eggs, free ones, and I'm queuing to get one," she said.

It was a stupid fib. But Grandma went along with it.

"That sounds lovely," she said, "I think I'll have an egg myself."

And she made her way to the end of the line.

A policeman was working his way down, questioning the whores. When he reached Grandma, he looked puzzled.

"You're about a hundred," said the policeman. "How do you do it?"

"Easy," said Gran, "I take out my dentures."

Kingsley stopped writing. "I've heard it all before," he said.

"I have one more tale about my grandmother," I said, "would you like to hear it?"

"Very well."

So I told him about the accident with the goat.

Riding strapped under a goat one day, I became trapped when the animal caught one of its forelegs in a cattle-grid. It lurched forward, trapping my face beneath its hairy chest. Luckily a group of island women happened by.

"I'll get help," said one of them, "the rest of you try and lift that goat off the poor lad."

They pulled at the goat, but the animal just screamed in pain. Its leg was firmly trapped between the bars of the cattle-grid.

"I hope that's not my man under there," said the first. She lifted my kilt.

"No, it's definitely not my man," she said, after examining my penis.

The second did the same thing. She handled my hairless little organ. "It's definitely not mine either," she declared, relieved.

The third woman—her voice was unmistakably my grand-mother's—lifted my kilt, tasted me, manhandled me to erec-tion, pumped sperm from my cock, made cheese with it, ma-tured the cheese, put it on the market, won a Queen's Award for Industry, and retired peacefully to the big house on the hill.

"Girls," she exclaimed, "he's not even from our island!"

24

The countryside was speeding cheerfully by. The Murderer, the Molester and I would soon return to the city to commit our crimes. But for now we were enjoying an afternoon out.

"I feel so safe on this train," sighed the Murderer.

"How can you say that, knowing that a murderer might be in our midst?" demanded the Molester. "Have you forgotten the young girl, the blood, the locked door?"

"Have you forgotten that I'm a murderer myself?" said the Murderer. "Think of it this way: the chances of there being a murderer on this train are low enough. But the chances of there being two murderers on the same train are almost non-existent."

"And the moral is, always travel with a murderer," I laughed, clapping the Murderer heartily on the back.

"I've told you never to hit me like that," said the Murderer.

"Concealed weapons," explained the Molester.

"I hear you have one or two yourself," I chuckled, gesturing a knee to the Molester's groin.

We all laughed.

"Still," said the Murderer, "it's nice to be safe. The way to live long and live well is to stay safe."

"I can't agree, my dear fellow," said the Molester. "Danger is what keeps us on our toes. Danger keeps us safe. The way to live a long time is to live dangerously."

"The Molester is right," I said, slightly pompously. "Negotiating danger is much safer than trying to eradicate it. No matter how hard we try, there will never be a world without danger. Better, then, to face it, and, by constant exposure, to come to know danger like a friend."

The Molester nodded. "It's safety that's truly dangerous," he said. "I hate safety. It's for sheep," he said, nodding at a passing flock.

"Are you telling me those sheep out there are in danger?" asked the Murderer. "Is there danger in numbers?"

"If there were," replied the Molester, "those sheep would be safe. No, there's safety in numbers, and that's what's so dangerous."

The Murderer looked perplexed.

"So if I introduced danger to those sheep in the form of a fox or a wolf, I would be helping keep them safe?"

"You would be doing them a great service," said the Molester.

I nodded. "You would be introducing the very essence of safety into their midst," I said.

"But if living dangerously helps you live a long time because it keeps you safe," said the Murderer, "we're back to my original proposition: that the way to live a long time is to stay safe."

"Yes," said the Molester.

"Exactly," I confirmed.

"But that's just what I started by saying," spluttered the Murderer. "And you both disagreed!"

"We only disagreed because there wasn't enough danger in your definition of safety," said the Molester.

"But I didn't offer any definition of safety at all!" the Murderer protested. "How can you disagree with an unstated definition?"

"On the contrary," said the Molester, "how can you agree with an unstated definition?"

The Murderer sighed.

"You clearly implied," I said, "that safety is good because it's safe. And we disagreed because we believe that safety is good because it's dangerous."

"Precisely," said the Molester. "We disagreed because we believe that danger is good because it's safe."

"But that means you're saying that safety must be good because it's safe!" said the Murderer.

"That doesn't follow at all," said the Molester.

"Quite," I agreed. "That kind of thinking is, in fact, highly dangerous."

"So it must be safe!" shouted the Murderer.

"Tickets, please!" said the ticket inspector, a pale young girl.

25

Troubled by an evil spirit which haunted the sauna in the grounds of our farmhouse, my father called on our old family friend, the Reverend I. M. Jolly, to perform an exorcism.

Since the spirit only appeared when the sauna was in operation, Jolly and my father removed their clothes and entered the wooden shed together. My father sprinkled holy water on the hot coals and the two men discarded their towels (though Jolly kept his dog-collar attached) and sat on the wooden benches naked, steeping in the deep heat.

It was a peculiarity of this evil spirit that it could only be apprehended through the nose. Soon enough a foul odour began to permeate the sauna. It was a rankly offensive blend of sulphur and Stilton—the ghost of lunch, you could say; for the two men had been sipping red wine and eating Stilton cheese at the end of a meal which had set the dining table heaving.

The ghost of lunch was quickly wafted on a humid convex to the hut's ceiling, where it hovered malignantly, taunting the naked men below, haunting their nostrils. It also attracted several houseflies, which began to fly around the sauna hut excitedly.

"There it is, Vicar!" exclaimed my father. "You can smell the evil spirit now, I am sure. The question is, how can we banish it?"

"I certainly can smell it," said Jolly, wrinkling his brow. "Remarkable how the spirit has disguised himself as a low, noxious human emission. Yet in this we see the cunning of Satan. It is his wont to disguise himself as anything low, foul and obnoxious. The ghost of lunch, for instance."

Despite the great heat of the chamber, the two men shivered, and a little more of the evil ectoplasm escaped from my father's behind with a "parp."

"I hope you can cast him out," said my father, "for, while he lurks here, nobody will join me in this sauna. I shall grow lonely."

"There is a sure way to banish this fiend," said Jolly, "though I fear you may not like it."

"What is that?" asked my father.

"We must trap Satan in hell," replied the minister.

"And how?"

"With a cork."

"I see."

While the Reverend I. M. Jolly screwed a large cork into my father's rectum, he told the sprawling man a story.

There was once an antiques dealer, he said, who was passing a butcher's shop when he almost tripped over a cat eating a human hand from a fine porcelain dish. Looking more closely at the dish, the dealer ascertained that it was from Tang

Dynasty China, and extremely valuable. He went in to speak to the butcher.

"Is that your cat outside?" he asked.

"The one eating the human hand?" asked the butcher. "Yes, that's my cat."

"Would you be prepared to sell him to me?" asked the dealer.

"I suppose I might, if the price were right," mused the butcher. "But why are you interested in that mangy beast? There's nothing special about him."

"Oh, nothing special at all, you're right. He's a very ordinary cat indeed. I just took a fancy to him, that's all. He . . . he reminds me of a tabby I once had, and loved dearly, a tabby who died."

"In that case," said the butcher with a cruel laugh, "I'll double the price! You can have him for two hundred."

It was a ridiculous price for a cat, but a bargain for the Tang dish. The dealer agreed, reached for his wallet, and handed over the sum.

"I think you'll find him very easy to care for," said the butcher, licking his fingers and counting the cash, "except for one thing. He's rather fussy about his food. He only eats human hands."

"I see," said the dealer. The cat's diet was the last thing on his mind. "You don't mind if I take his dish too, do you? He seems accustomed to it."

"Oh, I can't let you take that dish," said the butcher. "It's been in my family for years."

My father, prostrate on the sauna bench, snorted. Jolly continued.

The dealer was crushed. "Oh come on, I've just paid you two hundred, man, give me the dish, for pity's sake!"

"Sorry, I can't. That's my lucky dish. I've sold six cats this week alone!"

The dealer saw that he had been duped, and left the shop in a rage, banging the door behind him. The cat, though, seemed to recognize his new master. Gripping the human hand between his teeth, he began following the dealer down the street.

"Shoo! Shoo!" said the dealer. But the cat followed him faithfully, like a puppy, with the human hand dangling from his teeth like a slipper.

The antiques dealer turned corners, climbed stairs, changed direction, threatened the cat, kicked at it, but to no avail. The animal kept following him, just a step behind.

On a quiet street—the dealer and the cat were the only pedestrians—a policeman suddenly stepped out of a parked car and blocked the dealer's path.

"Excuse me sir, is that your cat?" he asked.

"No," said the dealer, "he's been following me ever since I passed a butcher's shop a few blocks back. It's very annoying. I've done everything in my power to shake him off."

"Did you notice that the cat is carrying a severed human hand in his mouth?" asked the policeman.

"No . . . I mean . . . yes, I did notice, how could I miss it? It's bloody sinister, isn't it? You need to question the butcher about that, not me. He's the cat's owner. Here, I'll take you to his shop."

And the dealer led the policeman to the butcher's shop, with the cat trotting along behind, the hand still hanging from its mouth.

The precious bowl had vanished. Inside, the butcher was hacking at a joint of meat.

"I wonder if I might ask you some questions," said the policeman. "Is this your cat?"

"It's not my cat," said the butcher, "it belongs to this gentleman here. I noticed it trotting along the street behind him not half an hour ago."

"That's a lie!" shouted the dealer. "He's not my cat! You sold him to me!"

"If I sold him to you, he must be your cat!" said the butcher. And to the policeman he added: "You see how his answers contradict themselves!"

"And the human hand?" demanded the policeman. "Got an explanation for that?"

"No," said the butcher.

"Yes," said the dealer. "I believe this butcher has murdered someone and is keeping the body in his cold room. You must search it, officer!"

"Very well," said the policeman. "Show me the cold room!"

The butcher indicated the cold room and followed the two men in, wiping his cleaver on his apron. A few minutes later he emerged with four fresh human hands. He dropped three into the freezer and threw the other one to the cat.

"You are a fussy pussy," he said.

"That's a very charming story," said my father, as he straightened up, "and this cork is more comfortable than I thought it was going to be."

"The exorcism is complete," said the Reverend Jolly. "It is my belief that you won't be troubled by that evil spirit again."

The reverend took a small glass of sherry before departing. My father took the opportunity to tell him a little story about his brothers, The Irishman and The Scotsman.

In later life, The Irishman had grown rather deaf; the banging of hunting guns had finished his ears. The two brothers were living together at that time on Summerisle.

One day in late autumn they caught the ferry to the mainland to attend an agricultural fair. There they happened to come across an old man who had lived on Summerisle a long time ago. He was rather a disgraceful old wretch, but he seemed delighted to meet them, and began to reminisce enthusiastically about life on the island.

"I remember the peat bog, where we used to lie hidden in the high reeds and watch the young girls as they bared everything in the stream," chuckled the old man.

The Scotsman laughed.

"What's he saying?" asked The Irishman.

"HE SAYS HE REMEMBERS THE PEAT BOGS!" said The Scotsman, shouting directly into the deaf man's ear.

"And I remember the wonderful shaggy orange highland cows," the old lizard continued, "and how we used to fuck them up the arse!"

"What's he saying now?" demanded The Irishman.

"HE SAYS HE MISSES OUR DEAR OLD HIGHLAND COWS!" shouted The Scotsman.

"And, best of all," exclaimed the withered old lecher, "I remember that wench on the square, the one with the quiffed fringe, who gave us all such unforgettable blow jobs."

"What? What was that?" demanded The Irishman.

The Scotsman hollered: "HE SAYS HE KNEW MOTHER!"

"Very nice, very nice," said the Reverend Jolly. "I'm afraid I must be off now. Thank you so much for the sherry."

26

The Murderer, the Molester and I alighted at the familiar station—the beloved, deserted station next to the orchard. Blossoms blazed pink and white in the trees, which stirred in rows, sharply lit by the mid-afternoon sun.

The train had already pulled away, but for a while we stood there in a line on the platform, transfixed and transported by the beauty of the scene before us. Each of us, in that moment, relived some dear moment of his youth.

Presently, wiping away tears of joy, I turned to my two companions.

"My dear fellows, this is the place of rightness, the place of fertility, the place of waving rye and scarecrows. Here the green-fingered god sprinkles Bollgard upon the furrows, calling forth the fecund fullness, the deep health-giving wellness, of the life of the fields."

The Molester turned to me, his face wettened and radiant.

"Here a smiling lord of the fields prances through fresh leaves free of the pesky boll weevil," he said, as if speaking from deep within a trance. "Here man and plant and insect exist in harmony, and sperm blows freely upon the wind."

"Here," said the Murderer, inclining towards us, his face craggy with fierce Celtic emotion, "the good tree wool pushes forth strong and abundant, while the evil falls upon fallow ground, there to die."

"Gentlemen, let us visit the community seed bank and gather in outspread hands the kernel sperm of the good earth," I proposed. "Let us celebrate the great spiral of revival, and let us make a sacrificial offering to the bounty of the fountainhead."

We walked to the end of the station platform and climbed the small stile we knew so well. The air, as we crossed the brilliant pink orchard, was startlingly fresh. Around our heads, birds sang softly—the Meadowlark, the Black-billed Capercaillie, and the dove.

"The flowers appear on the earth," intoned the Murderer, "the time of the singing of birds is come, and the voice of the turtle is heard in our land."

"Ah," I said, "the Song of Solomon, in the King James rendering. Beautiful! But of course it's wrong—other translations have the line as 'the turtledoves sing in our land.' It's a foolish misunderstanding. Turtles don't make any noise. They have no vocal cords."

"Actually, turtles and tortoises do make noise," corrected the Molester. "I've heard tortoises fucking, and they make this buzzing, cooing sound." He began to make a silly guttural noise, which echoed off the trunks of the cherry trees.

"It isn't cooing," said the Murderer. "I've strangled a few of those reptiles. They grunt, they cluck, and, finally, they make a very pretty death rattle. The nicest one to kill, in my experience, is Bell's Hinge-Backed Tortoise. In strictly musical terms, I mean. You flip off its shell—hopla, easy, like flipping up the lid of a metal rubbish bin!—and it starts doing this orgasmic bellow."

And the Murderer produced a horrible braying sound that bounced back at us from the small cluster of wooden sheds we were now passing.

"That's as may be," I said, annoyed. "But Solomon wasn't trying to say that the Holy Land was full of the death rattles and orgasmic grunts of tortoises. If you go back to the original—"

The Molester interrupted. "Hey," he hissed, beckoning us over to one of the small sheds, "come and see this!" As we approached, he raised his hand to his lips.

Shielding our eyes to block out the sunlight, we peered through the small window into the shed.

Inside, immaculately arranged, we could make out the industrial power tools of a well-equipped do-it-yourselfer. There were diesel lawnmowers, brightly coloured garden spreaders, a yellow sawing table, an orange electric generator, two compressors, a rotary lathe, a submersible pump, a coil of hose, a bench drill, a packet of stick electrodes, three impressive gas heating reflectors, a welding arc and goggles, several brightly coloured rubber aprons with matching gloves hanging from the pockets, a quick-coupling air accessory kit, a shortwave infrared paint dryer, a nitrile gauntlet (for use with thinners) and a dust-free suction-feed paraffin spray-gun.

"Nice kit!" cooed the Murderer.

It was indeed an impressive set-up. Any man, looking at that, would instantly dream of long, happy, solitary afternoons painting, cutting, assembling and destroying things. Any *real* man, anyway.

"So where is the owner of these tools?" demanded the Molester.

"I have an inkling," I said. "Follow me!"

27

It was 3 A.M. I slipped on a pair of pink slippers and padded down the glass staircase to the kitchen. My father, Sebastian Skeleton, was sitting at the table, eating a piece of tongue. It may have been pig's tongue, calf's tongue, or even his own. He had it pinned between two moldy slices of Turkish bread. His face, lit by the bulb that hangs low over the kitchen table, wore an expression of foolish delight, and his glazed eyes swiveled like marbles. Following them, I discovered a fat death's head moth beating stupidly against the bulb. Suddenly Dad opened his mouth, flicked out a sticky whiplash, and caught the moth on the curled tip. Within seconds he had gulped it down.

I watched for a few moments more, turned, and made to return stealthily to bed. But Dad had seen me.

"Peter, come here!" he shouted, licking the grey remains of moth off his lips. "Why are you still up?"

"I can't sleep."

"Come here and I'll tell you a story."

I obeyed.

My father started telling me about something that happened to him when he was my age.

"I wasn't getting any, and I needed some," he began. "I noticed a nun who rode your grandfather's bus every day at the same time. I conceived a filthy lust for her, all the more torrid for her luminous purity. I asked your grandfather's advice on how to seduce her."

"Hmm," pondered Grandad. "That'll be a tough nut to crack. These nuns are married to Christ, you know."

But suddenly he snapped his fingers.

"Married to Christ! There's your answer! All you have to do is dress up as Jesus—you already look a bit like him, Sebastian!—and wait for her in the churchyard halfway up the hill. She passes the spot every day, on her way from the bus to the nunnery."

"The very next day I did exactly as Gramps had suggested. I got dressed up as a semi-crucified—but roguishly attractive—Christ in a bloodied white loincloth. When the nun passed, I called out to her:

"Psst! Sister, Sister! Psst! You! My daughter! My child! Come here!"

"My Lord!" exclaimed the nun, seeing it was Jesus. "What is it that you require of me?"

"I'd like you to suck my cock," said Jesus.

That's not the end of Dad's story—of course it isn't!—but quite frankly I need to stretch my legs, otherwise I'll fall asleep. So let's take a walk, shall we?

The nunnery is up the hill, the church halfway down, and at the bottom there's the road where the bus passes. Despite all this tranquil sanctity, there's something sordid about this spot.

Blackbirds sing, and you can see freshly-cut roses in the manse window. But the graveyard feels dirty. There are solid cowpats by the graves—cows must have broken in—and a used condom hanging from the hedge.

A linnet is singing, and rabbits play cautiously in the hedgerows. I love these tales when they're set in the countryside, it's a really refreshing break.

But here comes the bus. We must continue.

"I can see your Grandad at the wheel. Oh, wait, no, it's someone else today. Out steps the fucking nun. The bus pulls away. The nun climbs the hill, gets to the graveyard, sees the half-crucified Christ. That's me. I beckon.

"She asks what Jesus?—what I—want her to do?

'I'd like you to suck my cock,' says Jesus.

"The nun seems surprised, but answers, without hesitation, 'Very well, My Saviour, on one condition.'

'What's that?' I demand, somewhat tetchily.

'That you let me fuck you up the rear after,' says the nun.

"Well, I'm obviously a bit surprised at that, but I agree. We get down to business.

"After the deed is done I light a cigarette and say, 'Sister, I have something to confess. I'm not really Jesus.'

"The nun doesn't seem upset. 'That's okay,' she says, 'I'm not who I seem to be either. I'm your dad, the bus driver.' "

Peter steps out from behind the hedge. "Hello Dad, hello Grandad," he says.

"Time for bed," says Dad. "You're asleep already."

28

The brilliant afternoon began to cloud over now, and a spring chill spread through the air. April is the cruelest month! And it was only March.

I gestured the Murderer and the Molester to follow me across the yard. Walking on the raised petal path, we crossed the yard to the pottery shed and slipped in through the half-open door.

I showed my comrades the secret hole and we squeezed through into the goose shed next door. A ladder stood immediately to our right. One by one we scaled its frail steps. The Murderer was the last one to arrive in the cozy hay loft. In one hand he carried a delicate yakimono cup. On it I could see the image of a baby eating a mushroom.

"Did you steal that from the pottery?" I asked, annoyed.

The Murderer said nothing, but turned the rough-glazed vessel around in his hand, tracing with his thumb its bumps and irregularities. He seemed quite engrossed.

"I love blemishes," he said. "They make life more interesting, don't you think?"

All of a sudden there was a commotion in the goose barn down below. A man entered the goose shed, singing softly to himself. I immediately recognized my son, Peter.

I gestured urgently for silence and beckoned the men back into the shadows.

The Molester wiped a spider's web—still containing a living spider and several dead flies—from his face, trying hard not to splutter with disgust.

"Goosey Goosey Gander, whither shall I wander," sang my son, unbuttoning his trousers down below. Through two slats of wood I could see the goose now, bedded down in a hollow concave of straw. My stomach turned. I looked at the Murderer and the Molester. Their faces, too, were milk-white.

"Goosey Goosey Gander whither shall I wander

Upstairs and downstairs and in my lady's chamber . . ."

Peter pulled out his penis and began to spread the handsome goose's tail feathers. Raising his finger to his lips, he licked it and smeared his saliva around the plump bird's sex.

"There I met an old man who wouldn't say his prayers

I took him by the left leg and THREW him down the STAIRS."

The words received the extra emphasis of my son's thrusts, which seemed to penetrate deep into the innards of the bird. Rebecca flapped her wings and squawked, but barely resisted my son's penis. My face, craning down from the gallery, burned with recognition and embarrassment.

At that moment—my son was close to his crisis, his mouth stupidly open, his eyes foolishly shut—the double doors were flung open. Joan stood there, resplendent in an ornate kimono depicting silver foxes against a grey and green pattern, braided around the edges with flashes of gold thread.

"My wife," I whispered to the two witnesses. "There'll be trouble now!"

Below, Peter seemed to take the interruption in his stride. Ejaculating messily onto Rebecca's tail feathers, he cried out: "This is the pig I've been fucking!"

"That's not a pig, that's a goose," intoned Joan in the weird ceremonial tones of a Noh play.

"I wasn't talking to you," said Peter, his voice equally stilted and mannered.

My wife raised a calm, sinister white mask to her face, turned, and left. The doors swung shut and we could hear Joan swishing off down the elevated walkway.

A thin halogen film of cloud passed momentarily over the white disk of the sun, then everything in the goose shed was bright again. Below, there was no one to be seen. Peter and the goose had vanished.

"Wasn't that your fucking son fucking that goose?" asked the Molester.

"He is my fucking son," I replied, shamefaced. "But I'm also fucking his."

29

My father began to receive a series of anonymous and threatening letters. They said that, although no legal action would be taken against him at present, he was being watched (as if he didn't know that!) and that if he were to visit a certain psychotherapist (name and address supplied) he would find any eventual penalty for his immorality much reduced. His first instinct was to ignore this pressure, but when the letters eventually spelled out the alternative outcomes—a warning from the police versus a faked suicide in prison—he decided it would do no harm to comply.

And so he began twice-weekly sessions with Elaine Cranberry, who had an office not far from where we lived. Cranberry was a colour therapist who believed that specific combinations of shade and hue could be prescribed for particular mental problems. Her consultation room was like an ice-cream cabinet; the telephone was pistachio, the sofa melon, the walls caramel, and the desk cherry.

Cranberry began, in the first session, by asking my father to remove his shoes and lie down on the melon sofa. She then shot the names of colours at him and wrote down his first associations in a fresh spiral-bound notepad with a blueberry-coloured cover.

RED

murder

BLUE

police

PINK

innocence

BROWN

shit

ORANGE

carrot

TEAL

duck

BLACK

death

GREEN

My father was stumped.

"Aphid blood," he said at last.

"Now," said Cranberry, moving to the afternoon's serious business, "I want you to tell me a particularly traumatic episode from your childhood."

My father thought for a while, then began.

"I must've been about six. My father took me to Highdown Fair. He was running a regular coach service there while the fair was on.

"Well, at the fair he bought me a little white mouse. I was delighted with the pet, which seemed so small, so cute, so intelligent."

"It was white?" demanded Cranberry, craning closer.

"Yes, pure white."

"No other small patches of colour, say on the hindparts or underquarters?"

"Not that I recall," said my father. "At least, not until it started bleeding."

"How did that happen?" asked Cranberry.

My father told her how he had been playing with the mouse, letting it run up the sleeve of his coat, when suddenly a grey cat had pounced and made off with the animal between its jaws. The cat dived between two stalls, ran through a small hole in a fence, and sat a few metres away, toying with the mouse. Then, as my father and grandfather watched in horror, the grey cat ate the mouse whole.

"A grey cat, you say? That's unusual," said Cranberry. "Normally grey cats will play with their prey for hours. Only after exhausting all resistance will they start biting into the flanks of their small victim. Grey cats are incorrigible serial killers," she added. "They should, in my opinion, be locked up."

"A worse fate befell this one," said my father. "A black dog suddenly loomed out of a hedgerow and swallowed the cat whole."

"A black dog, you say?" said Cranberry. "They have certain particularities. Attacking a cat, a black dog will usually clamp its teeth around the beast's neck and shake it about from side to side until the spinal column is broken. Then it will wolf down portions of flesh from its victim's flank, sharing the spoils with other black dogs in its pack."

"Is that so?" said my father.

"Yes," said Cranberry. "Black dogs are pack animals, they kill in groups. They should collectively, in my view, stand trial for war crimes."

"One would certainly hope that these animals are one day held accountable for their crimes," agreed my father. "But in the event some sort of rough justice was done that evening, for the black dog was set upon by a stout wooden stick, and beaten to death."

"A wooden stick? On its own, without anyone wielding it?"

"That is correct. Just the stick. It cudgeled the black dog which ate the grey cat which swallowed the white mouse, the one my father bought me at Highdown Fair."

"Most extraordinary," said Cranberry, writing. "What colour was the stick?"

"Just an ordinary wooden colour. Until, that is, the fire came along and burned it up."

"A fire burned the stick?"

"Yes, a fire burned the wooden stick that beat the black dog that jumped on the grey cat who ate up the white mouse my father bought at Highdown Fair."

"And you're quite sure the cat was grey?"

"Positive."

"I'm beginning to detect a pattern here," said Cranberry, running a finger lightly along the bridge of her nose. "Let me guess what happened next. The wind got up and blew the fire—which was a vivid shade of orange—out?"

"Not quite. Along came sweet water and put out the fire which burnt up the old stick which beat off the black dog that jumped on the grey cat who ate up the white mouse—"

"Yes, yes, I get the picture," interrupted Cranberry.

"But no sooner had the water extinguished the fire than—as if from the great cloud of steam that went up—there suddenly appeared a great ox, and a thirsty one, for it drank all the water which put out the fire which burned up the old stick, which—"

"Yes, I see," said Cranberry, irritated. "No need to recap. And the ox was what colour?"

"I didn't notice. I had no sooner noticed the animal than a butcher appeared, brandished an ax, and slaughtered the ox which drank all the water which put out the fire—"

"Stop, stop! Wait, let me catch up! What colour was the butcher?"

"He wore a white apron."

"We aren't seeing much in the way of colour—real colour—in this tale," said Cranberry. "This is making my analysis very difficult."

"I'm sorry," said my father, "I'm simply describing events as they happened. Do you want to hear what happened next?"

"Very well."

"The angel of death came for the butcher who—"

"Wait! Wait! What colour was the angel of death?"

"Black. As black as the ace of spades!" roared my father.

"And no sooner had the butcher fallen than the Lord descended from the pinnacle of the skies and threw down the butcher who slaughtered the great ox which drank all the water which put out the fire which burnt up the old stick which beat off the black dog that jumped on the grey cat who ate up the white mouse my father bought at Highdown Fair."

Cranberry let him finish. "And what colour was the Lord?" she asked at last.

"Mint green," said my father.

To cheer him up as he paid the session fee—it was hefty indeed—Cranberry told my father a joke. It was about a client of hers whose penis was much too big—fifty centimeters long, in fact.

After sizing up the problem, Cranberry told her client to go to a particular pond in the forest where he'd find a talking frog.

"There's nothing we can do for you medically," she said, "but each time you can get this frog to say the name of a colour, ten centimeters will be reduced from your penis."

The client dragged his penis over to the pond, located the frog, and began asking him questions.

"What colour are you, frog?" he said.

"I'm green," said the frog. Immediately, ten centimeters were removed from the man's penis.

"Hey, this works!" thought the man. His penis now measured 40 cm. It was still too big.

"What colour are you, froggy?" he asked again.

The frog looked annoyed. "I just told you," he said, "I'm green."

The man's penis was now only 30 cm long. It was still a bit too big—20 cm would be optimal. The man decided to ask one last time.

"What colour are you, Mr Frog?"

The frog rolled his eyes. "How many times do I have to answer this stupid fucking question?" he demanded. "Green, green, green!"

Cranberry exploded with laughter, but my father looked slightly sad.

30

On the train back to the city—where we would commit the crimes of which we had been accused—the Murderer, the Molester and I discussed whether a man could be the son of his own son.

"There is a precedent," said the Murderer, a devout Catholic. "The Father, the Son and the Holy Ghost. Three in one. The Trinity."

"But in the Trinity, is the Son father to the Father?" asked the Molester.

"It's a chicken-and-egg question," said the Murderer. Both men glanced in my direction. I rolled my eyes.

"But I can tell you this," continued the Murderer. "The child is father to the man, and necessity is the mother of invention."

I thought about this for a while, watching an oast house crammed with hops passing the train window.

"If the child is invention," I mused aloud, "and his father is married to necessity—his mother—then invention is both his father's son and father. He's also his mother's father-in-law as well as her son. Which means that invention is the father-in-law of necessity."

"And child to himself," added the Murderer, rummaging fussily in the sack he had filled with industrial power tools looted from the shed in the cherry orchard. Inside I glimpsed the primary-coloured paintwork of compressors, a lathe, a submersible pump, a coil of hose, a bench drill, a packet of stick electrodes, three impressive gas heating reflectors, a welding arc and goggles, several brightly coloured rubber aprons with matching gloves hanging from the pockets, a quick-coupling air accessory kit, a shortwave infrared paint dryer, a nitrile gauntlet (for use with thinners) and a dust-free suction-feed paraffin spray-gun.

There was a long silence during which we watched an oast house—identical to the last one—pass.

"The Father, the Son and the Holy Ghost are on a plane," said the Molester. "Suddenly it begins to plummet towards the ground. They will surely perish, leaving a God-shaped hole in the universe. There's only one chance of salvation; the plane must lose weight. Each of them must throw out something they have with them."

"I'll throw out a cloud, because there are lots of them in Heaven," says the Father. And so he throws out a cloud.

"I'll throw out this nail hammered into my hand," says the Son. And, tugging ten centimeters of iron out of his wounded hand, he throws it from the plane.

"I'll throw out my winding sheet," says the Holy Ghost, pulling the garment off and tossing it out of the plane.

The jettisoning is a success; the jet stabilizes and is able to make a normal landing in Heaven.

When the Father arrives back at his throne, a great wailing and crying and gnashing of teeth greets him.

"Why the consternation, people of Heaven?" asks the Father.

"Dear Lord," say the people of Heaven, "while you were away a great cloud fell suddenly from the sky and enveloped us. There was an almighty crash. When the fog lifted, we saw St Peter lying stretched out on the ground, crushed by a bus."

"Crushed but not killed," remarked the Murderer, "for The Gatekeeper has eternal life."

The Molester continued, unperturbed.

"When the Son assumed his place at the right hand side of his Father's throne, some bad news awaited him too."

"Our dear Lord Jesus Christ," said the people of Heaven, "while you were away a ten-centimeter nail came flying down and blinded your mother the Virgin Mary!"

Finally, the Holy Ghost walked into Heaven. "I suppose there's some bad news for me, too?" he asked.

The people of Heaven cast their eyes down and said nothing. "Yes," came the voice of the Devil, booming up from Hell. "You're stark naked."

Outside, the landscape was becoming suburban. There were gardening allotments, and a greenhouse flashed uniquely.

"Gentlemen," I said, changing the subject, "you've both read *Crime and Punishment*, haven't you?"

Of course they had. It was one of the most popular books in the prison library.

"How do you explain Raskolnikov's magnetic attraction to his own apprehension and punishment?"

"It's very simple," said the Molester. "If he's punished, order is restored to the universe. Even if he has to die in the process, it's worth it. Some things are worth more than mere survival. Honour and order, for instance."

"We see something similar in Kafka," the Molester continued. "Justice and cosmic order can be achieved only with the extinction of the subject who desires them. The two realms are incommensurate. Josef K is attracted to his own fate, and moves towards it of his own free will. The door to the law is for him alone—but it will close before he can pass through it."

The Murderer looked incredibly bored.

"There is hope," said the Molester, pressing his fingers together in the shape of a cage or a church steeple, "but not for us. A single goose could bring down the heavens—or so the geese believe. But the heavens signify, simply, the impossibility of geese."

The Murderer yawned.

"When my mother was giving birth to me," he suddenly announced, "she suffered agonies. It just went on and on. The midwife, wondering when the hell I'd get born, snatched up the candle and looked below to see if there was any sign of a head poking through. My mother, who was a bit naive, told the woman to check her bottom.

"Sometimes my husband uses that entrance too," she explained.

Silence descended on the compartment.

31

One afternoon—to the intense surprise of my father, my sister and myself—our mother, Joan, turned up at the glass house. My father answered the door in his dressing gown, hastily tying up the cords that folded several metres of silk around his penis. Joan was in the company of her lesbian lover (also called Joan) and the small, prissy, impeccable lawyer Bernard Bernardson.

The three of them formed a frigid and severe classical frieze. My mother wore a blue Cretan diplax draped over a flower-patterned chiton poderes with tassels. Her lover Joan wore a diaphanous ampechonion gathered with a fringed velvet cord around her waist. Her naked body could clearly be seen beneath. Finally, the lawyer, Bernard Bernardson, wore a fibule-fastened chiton surmounted by a himation, itself topped off by a jaunty chlamys, worn in case of the eventuality of foul weather.

With an air of great gravitas, the lawyer Bernard Bernardson carried in his arms a complicated potted plant. A trail of small drops on the floor indicated either that the plant had just been watered, or that he had chlamydia.

"This is indeed a surprise," said my father. "Come in, all three of you!"

The procession crossed the threshold. All three turned briefly to acknowledge the recess containing my father's household god—a statue of Priapus in the act of weighing his own penis against a bag of money and finding the organ heavier.

"Take a seat," said my father when they arrived in the kitchen.

"We prefer to stand," said both Joans in unison, like the chorus at an Epidaurian tragedy.

"So be it. What is your business today?"

The ladies fell silent and the lawyer, Bernard Bernardson, now raised his voice and spoke with winged words.

"Let the gods witness that we have brought a potted plant," he said. "For fourteen days and thirteen nights we intend to wander sandal-footed on the tempestuous shores of Thrace, along that path of wind-vexed sand that runs between foaming sea and jutting peak, above our heads only the wild shrieks of seabirds." Here he inserted some lifelike bird sounds. "During our absence we wish you to tend the plant."

"You want me to look after a potted plant?" said my father. "I thought you had a sterner request. This I shall do with pleasure and the deepest sense of responsibility. I swear it by Zeus, by Apollo, and by Demeter."

The three guests looked from one to the other and nodded. The lawyer, Bernard Bernardson, placed the pot, dripping, in the corner of the window-ledge.

"Then let this be accomplished," chorused the three. "For now to the farthest verge of honour, where Right erects her throne, hast thou most firmly sworn. O Father, should thou fail to keep thy oath, this debt of guilt most surely shalt thou pay to the uttermost."

It was a menacing speech, especially when uttered in unison by three people.

"Word of honour," said my father, "this potted plant is safe in my hands. See you in two weeks, and have a lovely time in Thrace!"

And he ushered his sinister guests to the door.

Two weeks later, the strange party returned. Joan (my mother) was wearing a diplax hymation and powder-blue mantile in Thracian style. Joan (her lover) had on a double-girded pink chiton, kilted at the knee. The lawyer was naked, and left a clear trail of drops on the carpet behind him.

My father experienced a sudden flurry of anxiety on seeing them. He had completely forgotten to water the plant! He went to the corner of the window-ledge where he had left it. A withered brown clump drooped in the cracked soil of the pot.

"The plant is withered!" screamed my mother, running to the window. Joan (her lover) rent her garments. The lawyer rent his hair.

Bernard Bernardson now raised his voice and spoke with winged words.

"What do you have to say for yourself?" he demanded. "Did you not swear an oath, by Zeus, by Apollo and by Demeter?"

And, speaking with winged words, my father now offered the following range of defenses:

1. The plant had never been entrusted to him.

2. In fact, it was *his* plant.

3. The plant had been entrusted to him, but he had never promised to return it in good condition.

4. He had sworn to the gods to ruin the plant, and was simply fulfilling his promise.

5. There was nothing whatsoever wrong with the plant.

6. He wished he'd never borrowed the plant, it was withered from the moment he set eyes on it.

7. This species of plant is withered from birth and, thus, is wither-proof.

8. The plant withered despite his best efforts. It was beset by a plague of flies.

9. Withering is only bad because we are conditioned to think of it as such.

10. In fact, healthy green sprouting is the most painful thing for a plant to endure.

11. Healthy green sprouting is an abomination.

12. Withering—warmly welcomed by sensible plants—is "the new" healthy green sprouting.

13. Therefore withering is good, because healthy green sprouting is good.

14. On the contrary, healthy green sprouting is abominable, and therefore withering is abominable.

15. Nothing as bad as withering could have happened to the plant under my watch. Therefore it has not withered.

16. Healthy plants have gone out of fashion during your absence.

17. This is not the same plant you left me.

18. This is, nevertheless and despite appearances, a healthy plant.

19. Look, there, behind you! A kitten!

20. The plant has committed suicide.

"What do you mean, *committed suicide*?" said the lawyer, Bernard Bernardson, turning back to my father after seeking the kitten in vain.

"It was healthy right up until the last moment—in fact, I never saw so bushy, so full, so glossy-leafed and happy a plant! I was so happy with its progress that I offered special sacrifices to Cronos and Themeter!"

"And what were these sacrifices?"

"To Cronos I offered the plant's roots, and to Themeter its leaves," my father stated.

"To Themeter I offered the plant's inside, to Cronos its outside," he added.

"To Cronos I offered the plant's knees, to Themeter its stomach," he corrected.

"For Themeter I made a sandwich of the plant, for Cronos a garland," he elaborated.

"To Cronos I told only lies, to Themeter only the truth," he concluded.

Standing in a stiff formal pose, tightly composed as if for a photograph, a convenient ornament covering the lawyer's genitals, the visitors fixed my father with an icy glare, whisked around on the heels of their buskins, and were gone, leaving only a trail of drips.

32

The Murderer was essentially middlebrow in his artistic tastes; he once declared that there were few tales which would not be improved by the addition of the phrase "suddenly, a shot rang out."

In fact, so enamoured was he with this phrase—the salutary burst of adrenalin he experienced on encountering it never seemed to fizzle into apathy, no matter how predictably the spurious shot was unleashed into the narrative—that he used to insert it into his copies of classic books. The moment the phrase would occur—accompanied by its acrid whiff of gunpowder—marked the exact point at which the Murderer's pathetically short attention span had given out, and his lust for adventure taken over.

The Murderer's copy of *Anna Karenina*, for instance, began:

"All happy families are alike, but an unhappy family is unhappy in its own manner. Suddenly, a shot rang out."

His copy of the Holy Bible started:

"The earth was formless and void, and darkness was over the surface of the deep, and the Spirit of God was moving over the surface of the waters. Suddenly, a shot rang out."

His copy of *Ulysses* opened with:

"Stately, plump Buck Mulligan came from the stairhead, bearing a bowl of lather on which a mirror and a razor lay crossed. Suddenly, a shot rang out."

Proust's *À la recherche* begins, in the Murderer's version:

"For a long time I used to go to bed early. Sometimes, when I had put out my candle, my eyes would close so quickly that I had not even time to say 'I'm going to sleep.' And half an hour later the thought that it was time to go to sleep would awaken me; I would try to put away the book which, I imagined, was still in my hands, and to blow out the light; I had been thinking all the time, while I was asleep, of what I had just been reading, but my thoughts had run into a channel of their own, until I myself seemed actually to have become the subject of my book: a church, a quartet, the rivalry between Francois I and Charles V. This impression would persist for some moments after I was awake; it did not disturb my mind, but it lay like scales upon my eyes and prevented them from registering the fact that suddenly, a shot rang out."

(The Murderer seems to have had a higher tolerance for Proust than other writers.)

The peculiar and remarkable thing was that, in staging these interventions in other people's narratives, the Murderer made them his own. While his eyes continued to scan the lines of the text as they were printed, one sensed that his mind, spurred on by a sudden, urgent adrenal fizz, was racing ahead with scenarios involving idiosyncratic detectives, gory autopsies on the main characters, ballistics reports, the pursuit of maniacal, unambiguously evil culprits, confrontations throwing the narrator into mortal danger, and the final return of order to the world.

Passing a cinema, the Murderer never failed to stop and admire any poster featuring a gun. "Capital! Suddenly, a shot rang out!" he would exclaim, and enter the fleapit to watch yet another banal, formulaic thriller. His favourite national cinema was, of course, the American one. Here, for sure, ringing shots were never long in coming.

In the darkness of the theatre the Murderer would sit, fists clenched tight with anticipation, waiting for the first crack of a pistol. "Come on, come on!" he would whisper, to the annoyance of other patrons, "come on, my beauty!"

If no shots rang out within the first few minutes, the Murderer would begin to fidget. "The pace is slow," he'd mumble, "something had better happen soon or . . . or . . ." The threat was left unstated, but it was a serious one. The Murderer had been known to carry a real pistol into a cinema, pull it out and fire it into the ceiling if his patience was tried. Several times he had been obliged to dash for the exit sign and run off down the street, with the hysterical sound of the cinema management calling "Police! Police!" behind him.

The Murderer's love of firearms in narrative didn't stop with Hollywood movies. He would insert gratuitous shootings into just about any story he told. It relaxed him and, in a sense, protected him from the dull complexity of the universe. Paradoxically, the constant reminder of violent death operated like the very opposite of a memento mori; it allowed him to gloss over death entirely. Evoking bullets penetrating human flesh was the Murderer's way of shielding himself from all sense of his own vulnerability.

It also exempted him from the responsibility of telling the truth. One day, for instance, the Murderer witnessed a crime. He was riding a bus. There were only two other passengers, an old lady and a teenager. This delinquent got up as if to dismount, pressed the button to open the bus door, then turned and grabbed the old lady's handbag, dashing off down the street with it.

The bus driver called the police—by this time they had already captured the boy, it turned out, as he tried to dispose of the handbag. When the two officers arrived, the Murderer was asked to make a formal witness statement.

"Well," the Murderer told the policemen, "the lady was sitting here, and the young man—wearing jeans, trainers and a purple hooded top with a white stripe down the arm—was here. When the bus stopped and the door opened, he grabbed her handbag and ran off. Suddenly, a shot rang out. The young man fell to the pavement, blood gushing from his head."

"Wait, wait," said the lieutenant, "there were no shots fired. The young man was not injured. We have him in the police car."

"I tell you a shot rang out!" insisted the Murderer, stubbornly. "I saw the thief fall. It was the old lady herself who shot him. A sting in the tail for the young miscreant, and an unforeseen twist in my tale! There are few stories which are not improved by a sudden shot ringing out."

The police decided the Murderer was psychologically incompetent to provide a witness statement, and released him.

The train was now arriving at its destination. Suddenly, a shot rang out.

33

We were making a family trip to the town of Dunbar. My father drove the vintage Bentley. Pointing it in the general direction of the east coast, he avoided the crowded A199 corridor and stuck, instead, to green lanes between knolls where we'd encounter only the occasional tractor or flock of sheep. His penis took up so much space—bundled like a gaudy pink and blue scarf over his shoulder and folded in layers on the back seat—that Luisa and I had to sit in the front, one on top of the other.

My father's monologue was as circuitous as the route he had chosen, but certain themes recurred. One was the joy of having a penis as vast as his own.

"The penis is mightier than the sword," he informed us, and sang in quivering baritone a snatch of advertising from the nineteenth century:

> They come as a Boon and a Blessing to men
> The Pickwick, the Owl, and the Waverly Pen.

Sexual pleasure, he informed us, was just like those pens—a boon and a blessing to mankind (which included womankind). Orgasm—however procured—was the greatest achievement of our species. "Never be ashamed of phallic values," he said. "Two thousand years ago, when our ancestors lived on this coast in rough wattle cottages, forts and castles, and fought the Norsemen who came to rape and pillage, life was worse in almost every way. The sword had not yet given way to the penis."

"But surely rape and pillage are the perfect penis values?" I challenged.

My father looked annoyed. "I'm not talking about the penises of others," he said. "It is our own penis which must prevail. When that happens, the Golden Age will be attained."

We were skirting the coast now, and on our left the sea stretched blue and white to the horizon, framed by sky and gorse. I imagined Norsemen arriving from Norway in longships with ferocious faces carved into the prows, Norsemen who planned to burn Dunbar to the ground and inject their DNA into the local women. And from that DNA would eventually spring monsters like Dad.

"Those people in far-distant millenia knew orgasm just as we do. Perhaps they lay fucking on this very harbour wall," said my father, tugging on the handbrake and packing his penis into a rucksack while Luisa and I lugged the picnic hamper out of the boot.

"Of course they had a robust pagan religion which put the important things—the sun, the seasons, crops, community rituals and fertility—at the centre of everything."

We spread a blanket out near the lighthouse and settled down to eat. As gulls wheeled overhead, scanning us with beaded eyes, my father pulled from the rucksack's outer pocket his well-worn copy of *Copulating Gorillas at Longinch*, a collection of poems by his old enemy Scotty Morocco. It was an ingrained habit of his to criticize these poems at every opportunity.

"Read this," said my father, stabbing at a passage and handing me the shabby book. He began to cut slabby sandwiches—white Milanda bread filled with a pink layer of processed salmon paste—into neat triangles.

While Luisa poured tea from a thermos flask, I read, for the umpteenth time, from the collection's title poem:

> Picking at ticks and fleas he's no ape Valentino,
> Is he?
> It's a scene that Sartre could have used to show
> Domestic misery.
> She's not much better, wearing slippers, all unwanted
> Intimacy;
> Bald arse sagging like a sack, a fat ape slag,
> Isn't she?

"It's so, so bad," chuckled my father, shaking his head. "Go on!" I read:

> He licks her hairy tits forensically, she cups his balls then
> Gradually,
> He licks then fucks her (sooner him than me!) up the
> filthy rear, and
> Frenziedly
> Ejaculates, while all the while the monkeys clap
> (The fucks)
> Enthusiastically.

"Now," said my father, stuffing his mouth with white and pink food and washing it down with a swig of tea, "tell me what's wrong with that poem? Eh?"

"It's obscene?" I ventured.

"No, that's the best thing about it!" roared my father. "Didn't you learn anything last time? Try again."

"What's wrong is just that it's a poem by Scotty Morocco and Dad hates Scotty," interjected Luisa, cattily.

"Shut up!" Dad bellowed.

"Is it the scansion?" I ventured, trying to remember what answer had placated him last time. "Bad scansion?"

"Nothing to do with the form," said my father, chomping on Milanda.

"I know, monkeys are not apes!" I cried.

"No, it's not that!"

"What's wrong with it, then?"

"I'll tell you what's wrong with it," said Dad. "The whole bloody attitude behind it, that's what. Examine the presuppositions! The hatred for sex! The disdain for orgasm! It's full of hate, hate for life."

"I suppose it is," I said. I was annoyed, though, that my father seemed to think there was just one right answer—his. This was typical.

"Dad, do you want to hear a conundrum?" I asked.

"Okay, tell me."

"Well, there was once a hermit who never left his home. Nobody visited him, except the people who brought food and supplies, but even they didn't come in. One stormy winter night an icy gale whipped up. The hermit had some kind of nervous breakdown. He climbed the stairs, turned off all the lights, and went to bed. The next morning, several hundred people were dead and it was all his fault. How did it happen?"

"That's easy," said my father. "After turning off all the lights, the hermit went out sleepwalking and killed several hundred people with a 5.45mm Kalashnikov AK-74 assault rifle."

"No," I said, "that's not what happened. Try again!"

"He picked them off from a window, with an air rifle?"

"No!"

"Ah, I see," said Dad, "it's a trick question. You didn't say he climbed the stairs in his own house. In fact, he climbed the stairs in everybody else's house, locking hundreds of residents out in the storm. They all died of exposure."

"Wrong again. He was a lighthouse keeper who turned off the light."

I smiled triumphantly, but Dad looked unimpressed. "I preferred my answers," he said.

"Of course you did," sneered Luisa.

"Shut up!" my father snapped. "The exercise is clearly designed to test lateral thinking. Yet my answers demonstrated much greater imaginative prowess than the correct solution."

"Okay, Dad, here's another. One dark, stormy night a couple are in a car driving fast through a foreign city. The car breaks down and the husband has to go and get help from someone who can speak his language. He's afraid to leave his wife alone in the car, so he winds up the windows and locks the car before leaving. When he returns the car is in the same state he left it in, but his wife is dead, there's blood on the floor and there's a stranger in the car. Explain what happened."

"Well," explained Dad, "the car broke down because the husband crashed it, killing his wife. The stranger was a policeman, investigating the crash. The man had been afraid to leave his dead wife alone because the area was a notorious necrophilia black spot."

"A necrophilia black spot?" asked Luisa. "What does that mean?"

"It means a place where there are a lot of people living who like to fuck dead people," explained my father.

"Are they marked with traffic signs?" asked Luisa.

"No, you just have to know about them through gossip and hearsay," said my father. "But when you reach such a place, well, even the policemen aren't above suspicion. Everybody is a potential necrophiliac. This officer was already fumbling with the dead woman's clothes."

"No," I said, "no, top marks for imagination, Dad, but that's not right. The wife was about to give birth. They were on their way to a hospital. While the man was fetching help the baby was born, but the wife died in childbirth."

"You're an incredibly boring person," said my father. "How you could be a son of mine I just don't know."

My father and I were leaning over the harbour wall, looking for fish in the water below. Nearby, an old man in a flat cap was dipping his rod, in a desultory manner, in the harbour water. Further along, sheltered from chilly sea zephyrs by the suntrap of the high wall, two little boys played with a portable game console. Up in the lighthouse the skeletal keeper watched us, rubbing his eyes.

Tiring of the pier, we headed inland, climbing through a small valley between two hills. An orchard in that tight place heaved obscenely with fruit. A postman on his bicycle passed a patch of purple foxgloves which waved their big overripe heads about in the breeze. A little girl, walking home alone from school, triggered a wave of anxiety in us all.

We entered a cottage with roses around the doorway. Inside was a plump country lady chopping apples with a long and pointed knife.

"Sit down," she said, welcomingly. It was impossible not to gaze at her massive breasts jiggling about as she chopped the fruit on the rough wooden block. All three of us ogled them quite openly.

"Would you like a big slice of apple pie?" the lady asked, as though she'd been expecting us.

We nodded. She was generous.

As she pulled some hot pie out of the oven and lashed it with thick jets of cream, the lady began to tell us a story.

"There were three mes," she said, "on an expedition in search of the source of the Lumbeezee River, deep in the jungle."

"Three yous?" echoed my father, puzzled, waving aside clouds of cream steam.

"Yes," said the lady. "The over me, the me, and the under me." Luisa blushed slightly as the lady pronounced the words "under me."

It was an odd story, but the lady continued it, placing three hot bowls of sweet white food in front of us.

"Suddenly the three mes were surrounded by an owl."

"Surrounded by an owl?" asked my father, his consternation growing. "How so?"

"Have you never been surrounded by an owl, when there are three of you?" asked the lady.

"No," said my father.

"It can happen in the twinkling of an eye. The mes are small, and the owl is large. Huge, in fact."

"Very well, go on."

"So the owl told the mes that he intended to use our lovely skin to make a leather boat with."

"A leather boat? Do owls use leather boats?" demanded Luisa, picking up on my father's skepticism. "Don't you mean a feather boat?"

The lady looked scornful. "Do I look as if I have feathers?" she said.

"Hush, Luisa, we're guests in this place," said my father, somewhat hypocritically. "So what did the three yous do?"

"I'll tell you, too-whit too-whoo!" joked the lady, whose breasts continued to wobble even when she was no longer chopping.

"The first me—the over me—pulled out a gun and shot myself in the head. 'You will not capture me alive,' I said to the owl. Before I pulled the trigger, that is."

"But why didn't you just shoot the owl, if you had a gun?" I demanded.

"Hush," said my father, "let her finish before raising that sort of logical objection. You must learn to keep an open mind until you are apprised of all the facts."

"Thank you," said the lady. "The second me—the me—then followed suit. I took out a knife and severed my jugular vein, right where it joins with the neck."

"A difficult feat," said my father, tut-tutting and shaking his head. "And the third you?"

"I was just coming to that," said the lady. "There was a huge fountain of blood, then the second me crumpled to the ground. The third me—the under me—grabbed the knife from the dying second me and began to hack and stab little punctures in my body, here and there, seemingly at random."

"What are you doing?" demanded the owl.

"I will be the leather for no owl's boat!" screamed the under me.

We all laughed politely—it seemed to be expected. Questions, though, remained.

"Do you mean that, when skinned, the punctured under me would sink the owl's boat?" asked my sister.

"Exactly," said the lady. "With all those holes in my under body, I would make a very poor leather boat indeed. I would surely capsize, drowning the owl."

"But owls can fly," said my sister. "Wouldn't it have been better to plunge the knife into the owl's heart?"

"Yes," I concurred, "or to shoot it in the face?"

The lady looked flustered. She flushed deep red and the room filled with the overpowering smell of her perfume.

"It's all very well to think about such things afterwards," she huffed. "I'd like to see what the three of you would do in the heat of such a terrible moment."

"Well," said my father, "at least one of the three of you lived to tell the tale."

"Can I interest you in some crafts?" the lady asked as we licked the last of the cream off our spoons.

"No," said my father, "I think we'd better be getting on our way. I see the sun sinking at the top of the valley, between the two hills."

"So it is," said the lady, gazing up at the three orbs. "We do have accommodation upstairs, I can make up three beds if need be."

"Thank you all the same, but we really must be going," said my father, ushering us back through the rose-blown door of the cottage.

On our way back to the harbour we passed the flattened corpse of the little girl, lying on the roadway. A car must have passed over her. Wolves had then, said my father, probably licked dry the juiciest parts of her remains.

34

It was already dark when the train, with a serpentine hiss of brakes, pulled into the city's central station. The Murderer, the Molester and I brushed the last cherry blossom petals from our jackets as we walked briskly through the station concourse. We were men with a purpose now. Three men, in fact, one carrying an enormous sack of stolen power tools on his back.

It was the Molester who set the pace. His crime was first. He led us across streets jammed with cars to the light-rail suburban link station. Soon, tickets in hand, we sat in a row on the narrow, shabbily-upholstered seats next to misanthropic commuters reading newspaper crime reports and murder mysteries. Aware that these suspicious-minded people might be memorizing details about us for future police reports, we tried to make our faces as identifiable as possible. We wanted, more than anything, to be picked out correctly in identification parades, in order to be given the punishment we had already received, and would shortly deserve.

The station in question arrived—an unimportant one, at which few commuters disembarked—and the Molester signaled silently that we should alight. Walking a few paces ahead of us, he turned right, then left, then right again, then straight for a while. Identical streets with small gardens succeeded each other. Only the lighting changed, getting dimmer and dimmer as we left the station further and further behind. One had the impression that there were bogs or swamps nearby; a light mist was visible in the feeble effluent of the sodium lights, and a smell of dank, stagnant water rose to the nostrils, tightening the throat.

Halfway down the street the Molester made a decisive gesture. We had arrived at the house. It was mostly dark, but along the side wall, parallel to the shingle drive, a window was lit—the window of the young girl's room. The Molester glanced up and down the street, saw that no one was there, motioned for us to wait by the gate post, removed his shoes and crept stealthily up to the window.

The Murderer set down his sack, and I half hid myself behind his hulking frame.

We could see the room just enough to distinguish the form of a young girl sitting before a mirror, brushing her long hair. Her lips seemed to move, as though she were talking to her reflection. I could see the Molester, a shadow mingled now with the ivy framing the girl's window, fumbling with his flies as he gazed at the girl's face, her lips, her hair. I imagined his small penis (I had seen it in the prison shower room) exposed to the damp evening air, primed, hard and shabby, ready to shoot a hot jet of human seed into the flower bed.

His furtive motion was interrupted by the girl. She had grabbed a tabby cat and was opening the window, apparently to release the beast into the garden. The Molester took his chance to elevate his crime from a minor, insignificant one to something much more ambitious. As soon as she had released the cat, he caught hold of the girl's wrist and hoisted himself in through her window.

We moved a little closer, taking little care to prevent our feet scrunching on the gravel. The Molester's first action, on arriving in the room, was to cover the girl's mouth with his hand. The girl seemed surprisingly calm. She had obviously taken a sensible decision to obey the intruder rather than risk harm. She sank to her knees and, from where we stood, all we could see was the Molester thrusting his hips backward and forward for several minutes. It was something he must have rehearsed in a hundred dreams.

"He is certainly not robbing now," nodded the Murderer, resting a foot on his sack of implements. "These pleasurable pelvic thrusts are prepaid. He has already served the time and paid the price for them. Society—in the form of that young girl—is repaying its debt to him."

At that moment, three things happened almost simultaneously. The voice of the girl's mother rang through the house, calling her daughter. The Molester convulsed in an enormous spasm, buckled at the knees. And a car pulled into the driveway, the car containing the girl's father, returning from work. It must have been a busy day; he hadn't even changed out of his policeman's uniform.

It would be a misfortune indeed to be arrested as accessories to another man's crime without having had the chance to commit one's own. The Murderer swung his sack onto his back and together we dashed into the bushes, leaving the Molester to lunge clumsily over the window ledge, jump almost onto the back of the tabby cat, and stagger up the gravel driveway, his trousers around his ankles, his drooling penis garishly illuminated by the astonished policeman's headlights. The little girl ran out behind him, sperm spilling from her mouth.

"Daddy, Daddy," she slurred and burbled, "arrest him, Daddy! This criminal molested me! Arrest him!" The seed made her sound drunk.

The policeman threw the confused Molester over the bonnet of his car, reached for his belt and clicked handcuffs onto our friend's spermy hands.

"A molester, eh?" he said. "I'll see you get ten years for this!"

The Murderer and I cut across the neighbour's garden, climb a fence, scale a fragile greenhouse which begins to collapse under our weight, find ourselves on a parallel street which seems almost identical (there's even another house with another young girl sitting at the window, brushing her hair), run along an alley and emerge onto an abandoned fairground site.

We dart between the abandoned tents, find an exit, and begin to walk, as naturally as we can, behind a woman with the distinguished bone structure and poised movements of an actress.

The station isn't far now. Unfortunately the Actress seems to be going there too. Each time we try to cross the street, she crosses it first. What if she thought we were following her? Should we linger beneath a lamppost—this crooked one here, for instance—to give her time to pull further ahead? But no, to stop like that would look even more suspicious. We must continue behind her.

The Actress has noticed us. She glances back in a casual way that contains the unmistakable look of anxiety. What if she should spot my missing ear? The Murderer's hunched sack-back and fearsome, craggy brow? These are certainly details she would remember, details she would be able to report to the police.

The Murderer and I cross the street and edge slowly past so that it no longer seems that we're following her. There's a canal leading to the station parallel to the main street. When we reach the stairs down to the towpath, we descend them rather than taking the lit street. That way we'll avoid alarming the woman. There's a smell of urine down here. Obscene graffiti and used condoms litter the walls and ground.

Imagine our horror, on this towpath lit only by chilly moonlight, to see the Actress again, walking in front of us! If she looks back, what will she make of two headless men holding hands? We clamber up a steep bank, swing over a fence, stumble clumsily through some garden beds, slink down the side of a house, and reach the narrow alley beyond. We disturb a cat—the same tabby the little girl released from her bedroom window, or a close relative. In the distance police sirens shrill.

Suddenly—tok, tok, tok!—the sound of a woman's high-heeled shoes is reverberating along this small corridor! We must hide, for what will the Actress make of two men who are only a raincoat, a pelvis, two cricket pads, and a stout cane?

The Murderer and I push ourselves into a cranny and stand very still on top of the sack, with our backs to the alley, waiting for the footsteps to stop. But when we turn around, she's there in the nook directly opposite, pulling down her underwear, squatting to pee! She will surely catch sight of two hidden, watching men who are only two pairs of empty trousers with four skeletal feet poking out the bottoms! Certainly she will assume the worst and panic!

There is no other choice; the Murderer must kill her.

His two bare white feet fly out of the shadows, but all that reaches the Actress's throat are ten detached toe bones, a primitive tribal necklace. As the toes scrabble and scratch her neck, she utters a horrible scream. It will echo long in my ears . . . but what ears?

35

My father became concerned by the rumours which were circulating at school about goings-on in the glass house. These rumours were not without substance—if anything, they erred on the side of caution. They were based on solid reports coming in from the lamplighters and the window-cleaners—and the books I was by now beginning to publish.

In order to avoid the kind of scandal which might have forced him—heaven forbid!—to correct his behaviour, my father decided to attack the problem at its root, its source. And so he not only condemned the whole idea of school, but set about reproducing it in every detail in the glass house. He was a consummate hypocrite. Or, as he preferred to put it, a dialectician.

A private tutor named Billy Plantagenet was engaged to impart to Luisa and me, at home, all the really important things we would have encountered at school. Billy was a flamboyant homosexual (as were many of the teachers at our school—indeed, Billy himself had briefly taught there) who had gone straight. Little by little—in fact, rather quickly, for he loved to ramble during lessons—Billy told us his story.

His life, it seems, had taken a distinct turn for the worse when his record label and his Moroccan boyfriend—a worthless piece of rough trade, and yet, at the same time, Billy insisted, a king among boys—had both dropped him in the same month.

Attempting to make the best of a bad deal, Billy decided to believe that he had quit music to concentrate on his personal life, and left his boyfriend to devote more of his time to music. As he explained in an interview—it was to be his last—with *Rock and Folk* magazine, an artist can never lose. For, even when he loses his lover, he surely gains the depth of experience and emotional profundity necessary to make the best work of his career. And even when he loses his record deal, he often finds, for the first time, the value of self-expression for its own sake, and the simple joys of life itself. His next album, he swore, would be his best.

Of course, it never appeared.

Nor, it seemed, were his chances of fucking attractive young boys improving. Swimming in oceans of self-justifying complacency, which both concealed and revealed even deeper oceans of misery, Billy Plantagenet began to drink heavily. Soon he began losing his hair and his looks. Typically, Billy welcomed the loss of his hair, and took to wearing a wig which reproduced it exactly. He welcomed the lines which began to appear on his face—they give a man character, he said—and yet slept in masks of cucumber face cream, injected himself with Botox, and applied, in every spare moment, a micro-massaging electric skin wand to the bags below his eyes.

Even when, in the mirror, Billy saw his craggy good looks eroding and a fat old prune standing where once had towered a magnetic sex god, he managed to find a silver lining in the cloud. "Now people will love me for who I really am," he reasoned.

Billy and my father were alike in many ways.

And yet, increasingly, "who Billy really was" was a drunkard, with the same stereotypical behavioural tics we see in drunkards all over the world. First they love you, then they want to fight you, then they love you again. And then they fall down.

There was only one solution: Billy would become a school teacher. Standing at the front of a classroom, he would bathe once more in the admiring attention of crowds of teenagers. But this time it would be even better. Instead of listening because they wanted to, these handsome, eager boys would listen because they had to! Instead of being a wanton entertainment, Plantagenet would have the full force of a respectable institution behind him. And instead of having to write songs, he could just spout educational-sounding rubbish off the top of his head.

This is pretty much the didactic technique he brought to the glass house when my father engaged Billy as our private tutor. His career as a school teacher had been short-lived. He had been caught buggering a North African girl in the pottery shed.

Summoned before the Head, Billy had argued that there were mitigating circumstances. Firstly, his natural proclivity, he said, was for boys. But, in a concession to conventional decency, he had in this instance chosen a girl. In an effort to avoid the scandal of pregnancy he had used her rear passage rather than the front one. And finally—this, he hoped, was the clincher—he had procured no personal enjoyment from the act, and was in fact delighted to have been caught *in flagrante delicto* by Mrs Dalloway, the chemistry teacher.

Mrs Dalloway had, in fact, said Billy, spared him any obligation to continue prodding into that joyless and barren cul-de-sac. He asked the headmaster to call Mrs Dalloway to his office forthwith so that Plantagenet could thank her personally—and, why not, the pupil too, who would confirm that she too had gained no pleasure whatsoever from the act. They could even re-enact the scene to prove the veracity of the account.

Naturally, the Head threw him out. "You have insulted the ethos of this school!" he shouted after the departing rocker. "Here we take the taboo of pupil-teacher sex very seriously indeed. It's basic—it structures everything we do. You have not only crossed that red line, but ridiculed and belittled the reward waiting on the other side. At the very least, you could have tried to enjoy it!"

And so Billy Plantagenet arrived at the glass house with his wig, his pot belly, his clinking briefcase, his fund of funny stories and his philosophy of life. For our first lesson, he encouraged my sister and me to imagine ourselves as rival advertising creatives awarded a briarwood-pipe campaign.

The lesson took place in Nao's room. Plantagenet banged down three identical pipes on the low kotatsu table.

"This is the Crepe, this is the Venue, and this is the Suitor," he explained. "These are the three models of briarwood pipe the manufacturer, Konig, wishes to differentiate. In your campaigns you must bring them alive with personalities of their own. I want you to work separately, in competition."

"But what are the differences between the three models?" my sister demanded.

"They are identical," said Plantagenet. "That's the challenge. Though in fact there *is* one difference. Can you tell me what it is?"

We picked the pipes up and turned them around in our small hands, but neither of us could see any difference whatsoever.

"I've already told you," said Plantagenet. "They have different names. And already that's an enormous clue as to the direction in which you must take your campaigns. Names mean everything. You do not have three plain wooden smoking pipes, but a Crepe, a Venue, and a Suitor. Konig has done most of the work for you."

"Those are stupid names!" burst out my sister. "The company must be idiots! Who would smoke a Crepe, or puff on a Suitor? Who would set fire to a Venue?"

I tended to agree. "Luisa is right," I said.

"No," corrected Plantagenet, "the client is right. Always. Now, divide into your two teams, and go and do your campaign brainstorming."

We slunk to opposite corners of the room and began to sketch our ideas on big sheets of paper. I was stumped, I must admit, and mostly played noughts and crosses with myself. After an hour, Plantagenet called us to outline our campaign strategies on the blackboard.

Luisa was first. She had decided to go with the absurdity of the names rather than fight it. She drew three figures on the blackboard, framed by three rectangles.

"This is a major television campaign," she said, "backed up by press and web. We have a ridiculous-looking man with a moustache in all three ads. His name is Monsieur Pipe. His life is very dull until he discovers new applications for commonplace objects around him. This is based on Guilford's Alternate Uses Test, a standard part of the battery of creativity research."

Plantagenet nodded his approval. Luisa was a smart girl, as well as possessing a prettiness which was nearly boyish.

"In the first ad we see Monsieur Pipe exhibiting 'oral restlessness.' He wants to put something in his mouth. This, of course, is based on the Object Relations School of psychoanalysis, pioneered in Edinburgh by Ronald Fairbairn."

I was beginning to grow irritated. It was clear Luisa's presentation would win.

"Monsieur Pipe casts about for something to put in his mouth. The first thing he finds is a crepe. As he lifts the crepe to his mouth, the screen wobbles in the familiar cinematic device indicating a dream sequence. The crepe turns into a briarwood pipe, the Crepe. He smokes it and smiles broadly."

"In the other ads, different instincts are appeased by the pipes," Luisa continued. "In the Suitor ad, Monsieur Pipe embraces the maid and is delighted to find her transformed into a reassuring briarwood pipe just as his lips touch hers. In the Venue ad, Monsieur Pipe, beaming with the glee only known to true arsonists, is about to burn down a magnificent theatre when it turns into a briarwood pipe. He lights it and puffs smoke into the air, tipping his hat at a policeman who saunters by."

Plantagenet was ecstatic. His trousers were around his ankles and he was masturbating furiously.

"That is an excellent solution, Luisa!" he gasped. "You have a wonderful grasp of the pillars of commerce. Now finish me off!"

I tore up my notes and flounced out of the room, followed by Luisa. We climbed the glass stairs to our bedrooms. Plantagenet, we knew, had the good fortune of being too fat to follow.

36

The Murderer, loping hunched at my side, seemed to have grown to twice his normal size. Incomprehensible syllables issued from his bulbous mouth, utterances of troublingly uncertain import. This was his hour, the moment of the Murderer's criminal epiphany, his horrid hosanna. Like the foul fog gathering around the lamps—the lamplighters were craning into them, increasing the flow of gas and removing a thick scum of moth-clogged spider's webs from within—an evil-smelling trepidation gathered in my breast as I saw the great, primal creature lumbering ahead of me towards the glass house.

Seeing the hunchbacked Murderer lurch by beneath them, the lamplighters began to sing out to each other, signaling in their own private language an obscene excitement. Something would happen soon in the glass house, something which they would photograph with small Japanese digital cameras, perched atop the lamp-posts on tiny portable tripods. This would be a horrible, historic day, and the lamplighters would bring word of it to the world.

The house seemed darker than usual. We knew it lay just ahead—our feet were already scrunching in the gravel of the drive—and yet nothing of its luminance could yet be seen. Instead, we sensed its presence in the form of an absence. It was a great dark expanse, the looming black hull of a ship in dry dock. An owl—I think that's what it was—rattled startlingly out of a rhododendron and skimmed our heads before winging off towards the forest.

An eldritch figure, surprising us both, staggered out of the fog. It was the lawyer, Bernard Bernardson. Lunging towards us dressed in a disturbed himation, the lawyer gibbered, on winged words, a warning.

"Stop! Do not enter the house!" said Bernardson to the Murderer, who had dropped his sack to the grass and was rummaging inside it.

With the super-competent, semi-automatic gestures of a skilled tradesman preparing for work, the Murderer pulled on a pair of protective goggles, some bright red, extra-long, heavy duty welding gloves, and a rubberized flame-retardant butcher's apron. Lighting three impressive gas heating reflectors and arranging them in a circle around the panicky lawyer, the Murderer connected the welding arc to its power pack and ignited its bright white sparking head.

"By Artemis," cried the lawyer, averting his eyes, "what is this?"

Without replying, the great brute drove the torch, from blade to hilt, into the lawyer's neck. Crumpling into the fog, Bernardson spoke then on winged words:

"Non victi sed vincendo fatigati!" he said, and, before he died, translated: "Not the victor, but the weary vanquished!"

A second man rushed up on the foggy lawn. "It's a lovely day tonight, sure enough!" came a familiar voice. It was the Reverend I. M. Jolly. I hadn't seen him in years.

"Jolly!" I cried, clasping the dear old fellow in a warm embrace. But as soon as my arms were around him, I felt a massive upward blow rending the man's frame. The minister sagged in my arms and slumped towards the gravel. "This is not entirely unexpected," he groaned, and fell lifeless to the damp soil. The Murderer stood behind, his torch sparkling pink with Jolly's blood.

"Isn't it pretty?" he cooed.

"Was that really necessary?" I demanded irritably. "That man was a good friend! He performed a successful exorcism on me once!"

"Murder is murder," said the Murderer. "You might as well question the wind, the sea, the moon or the fog."

And he turned towards the looming dark hull of the glass house.

37

Family holidays on Summerisle could get a bit dull, especially when the weather was bad. On really cloudy, wet days we'd pull on bright yellow sou'westers and make for the harbour, where Gracchus Hunter, the ferryman, would row us over to the nearby Isle of Bute.

Luisa and I hung like figureheads from the prow, craggy-faced Gracchus sat in the middle swinging the oars, and my father lurked on the boat's back bench, facing the receding coast of Summerisle. His enormous penis bobbed along in the foam of the wake, supported by three orange lifesavers.

There was just one reason to visit Bute: the Winter Gardens music hall. Here outlandish vaudeville entertainments—the relics of another age—could be seen: acrobatics, song-and-dance routines, brash comedy, slapstick. The manager of the Winter Gardens was a traditionalist, but also an experimentalist. Donald Farquar loved the traditional variety format, but believed that it needed new content to stay relevant to the times. Fresh blood, new faces, things never seen.

As showtime approached, a Victorian silhouette could be seen on the pier at Rothesay Harbour greeting arriving vessels. The silhouette had a pocket watch in one hand, a barometer in the other. This was Farquar. Low barometric pressure was his friend; he liked to describe rain clouds as "money clouds"; each speck of rain brought bigger crowds. Most of the visitors came by boat from adjacent islands.

"Farquar, you old fucker!" shouted my father, delighted, as we moored. The two men were old friends; they'd killed together in the war. Farquar hoisted my father up onto the pier and slapped his back heartily. "Got any new ideas for me, Rudolf?" he demanded (he called my father Rudolf, for reasons which escape me).

"As a matter of fact, I do," said Sebastian. "I've worked up a little family entertainment which might fit the late summer season."

"Excellent, come to my office and tell me about it."

Once my father had stowed his penis safely around his waist, we bade Gracchus farewell and walked up to the magnificent music hall.

Every inch of the Winter Gardens building was exuberantly decorated. There were stained glass windows, flock wallpapers sporting a dragon motif, elaborately carved bar cabinets, fancily framed photographs of the great music hall artistes of the past, and, above, chandeliers of vulgar opulence. The contrast with the sad, cheap and mean buildings that covered the rest of the Rothesay seafront—cottages, fish and chip shops, shabby newsagents, grim tobacconist-confectioners, a threadbare post office—couldn't have been greater.

Farquar stopped at the bar and ordered four pints of Guinness. He handed each of us a creamy-topped black glass and gestured us to follow him up the broad, red-carpeted staircase.

His office—a splendid room filled with crystal ornaments, chiming clocks, a crazy golf course and a model railway—overlooked the harbour. My father took a seat on one side of the massive mahogany desk, Farquar the other. We children, setting our Guinness on the floor after a gulp or two of the bitter black liquid, began to play with the model railway.

"So, tell me about your idea," said Farquar, after the men had exchanged small talk for a couple of minutes.

"You'll love it," said my father. "It involves the whole family, Grandma, me, the kids. Not Joan, of course."

"I'm all ears. Imagine I'm sitting out front, in the audience. The curtain goes up, your act begins. What do I see?"

"Well," said Sebastian, "the stage would be very dark as we came onstage. Grandma would arrive first."

"Mind she doesn't trip!" said Farquar.

"Oh, she's sure-footed as a panther!" my father said. The men both took a swallow of Guinness.

"The lights come up, Grandma begins to strip."

Farquar looked a little nonplussed. "Go on," he said.

"That can take as long as you like," said my dad. "She can milk the thing for grotesque laughs. We can have the band play some raunchy strip music as she gets her haggard old dugs out."

"That could be arranged," said Farquar. He leaned back and began stroking his goatee, his face slightly clouded.

"Okay. When Gran's naked, I rush out, naked too. I jump on Gran from behind and dry hump her, spattering her wrinkled buttocks with spunk," said my father, getting into his stride. "That's when the kids come on. They fuck each other, then I fuck each of them in turn, oral, anal, genital. Gran takes out

162

her dentures and sucks this one off . . ." (he patted my head) ". . . then a man dressed as a policeman runs onto the stage blowing his whistle. Instead of stopping, we push him between Luisa's legs and tug his trousers down. Then I truncheon him on the bonce with my dick for about five minutes, until he starts fucking the girl. When he comes, a huge bucket of sperm is tipped over us from above and the curtains swing shut as we writhe about in it."

Farquar looked thunderstruck. "And what do you call this act?" he asked.

"I can't think of a name," said my father.

They ran through this rigmarole every time they met. Only the details of the sex acts changed; each time they got just a little more lurid. In avant-garde vaudeville, this was axiomatic; you needed to go further to get to, essentially, the same place. Seventy years ago a joke about a Chinese laundryman steaming ladies' knickers might have sufficed.

"We do have an act a bit like that," said Farquar, drying his eyes. "Well, in the sense that it's a family act. The act's scato, not incest, though."

"Really?" said my father, blowing his nose with a thunderous "parp."

"Yes, they're Chinese. They play a family with two sons, one a swot, the other an idiot. Which is funny, because they really are a family with swot and idiot sons. They hold a big dinner party with lots of important guests. But since they're so ashamed of the halfwit son, they hide him "down a well"—which means, actually, in the orchestra pit. The idiot climbs down there. He begins to wail pitifully, says he's hungry. His mum waddles over and says they'll send him down some egg-drop soup later.

"Meanwhile, the swot son is pestering some of the guests. He's dancing around shouting 'I need to pee, I need to pee!' His mum takes him aside and says, 'Pee's a rude word, don't say that in front of our guests! In future, when you need to tinkle say, 'I want to sing!'

"The swot says 'okay' and goes off to finish his homework. When it's all done, he comes back down to the party. The governor of Chi-Chen is looking a bit green in the face. He's eaten and drunk too much. He lurches up to the edge of the stage, pulls down his trousers and pants, and releases the hot contents of his sick stomach into the orchestra pit in a huge explosion of diarrhea.

"Suddenly two voices rise up from the pit. 'Stop, stop,' they shout, 'that's enough egg-drop soup!' It's the idiot son and the second clarinetist. They're both getting slathered with shit.

"At that moment the swot son appears at the edge of the stage too. 'I want to sing!' he says, rummaging about inside his trousers.

'Okay,' says the Governor, by now an exhausted heap on the edge of the stage, his clothes half off. 'Come over here, boy, and sing in my ear.' "

My father roared his approval. "And what do they call that act?" he asked.

"It doesn't really have a name yet," said Farquar. "But it's making the orchestra pit pretty stinky."

38

The glass house felt abandoned inside; strange, muffled. Its once-bright, transparent surfaces had been deadened by the thick industrial felt—in varying shades of grey, flecked with red threads—someone had padded against each window and wall like cladding insulation. Where once the building had resembled a public library or swimming bath, now it seemed more like a yurt.

The Murderer approached his task in a highly professional manner. First he lit the site of the killing—the centre of the living room—with three Sealey fluorescent floor lamps mounted in bright yellow impact-resistant heads, each one standing on a yellow folding frame. This bathed the site in a milky-cold light with a correlated colour temperature (CCT) of approximately 6500 degrees Kelvin. These lamps are normally used for lighting colour-critical visual tasks in the printing and textile industries.

Meanwhile I began thwacking, with a Duo Vac Super Premium BTO-07C electric carpet beater, the suspended thick sheets of grey and brown felt behind which human forms were hiding. Great clouds of dust filled the air.

One by one, minor characters from this book began to emerge, coughing and blinking nervously in the harsh light. The sexologist Howard Kingsley was the first to wander into the triangular area demarcated by the three yellow-framed site lamps, rubbing his eyes. The Murderer felled Kingsley with a Trend C208X1/2TC Intumescent Cutter Set—an implement designed to help carpenters cut neat grooves into doors in such a way that they readily accept intumescent strips.

The teacher Billy Plantagenet was next. Looking sleepy, his rockabilly quiff all gappy and stringy, Plantagenet stumbled over Kingsley's twitching corpse and was impacted by the Murderer's Draper 12–16mm capacity Nut Splitter, designed for the safe removal of corroded or damaged nuts without damaging bolt threads.

"In many ways," said Plantagenet as he fell to the carpet, "this is the best possible thing that could have happened to me."

"The Draper Nut Splitter, featuring a forged medium carbon steel frame with enclosed head and chrome plate finish, is a thing of beauty," the Murderer called cheerfully across the room. He was a man in his element.

I agreed, raising my voice above the whine of the Duo Vac. The felt dust was making it hard to breathe: I pulled an acid-yellow Comfort 5 filtered dust mask over my face.

My beating raised Donald Farquar, the manager of the Winter Gardens music hall, Rothesay, Isle of Bute. The old codger looked a little disoriented, as if he'd been caught on the whisky or sleeping in the aisles. When the Murderer's Makita 2414NB 240 volt abrasive cut-off saw sank into his belly, Farquar looked thunderstruck.

"I wouldnae put it past you," he gasped, and died.

Nao the Japanese babysitter tiptoed by and was instantly dealt a death-blow from the Murderer's Dewalt Professional Chipping Hammer. "I am inexcusable," she said as she curled up tightly into a ball.

"Ideal for light demolition, surface preparation or chiseling grooves, channels and openings in brick, masonry and light concrete," explained the Murderer, adding, "Unique dust-sealing protection to prevent even the finest dust ingress into the mechanism."

Schlumm the Bad Gastein Librarian, in his demonic Klaubauf outfit, was on his hands and knees, examining Nao's blood-spattered graphic novel, when unexpectedly a 12-inch Stanley claw precision pry bar sank between his horns. Ideal for heavy-duty demolition, the pry bar (boasting polished bevel claws) was made of forged high-carbon alloy steel tempered for safety and long life.

"This is highly typical!" hissed the sinking Schlumm.

I began to feel slightly uneasy when a Black and Decker GT501 hedge trimmer felled Janaina, a plump girl who used to invite Luisa to pajama parties. If this buzzy saw—its specifications optimized for the trimming of bushes, hedges and small-leafed trees—could take the life of a young girl, were my own children safe? What would happen if Peter or Luisa themselves appeared at the site of killing?

The Murderer was cutting the beekeepers Bim and Spot to pieces using the contents of a pack of 100 Stanley hooked knife blades, specially pointed for penetrating and cutting sheet metal, in particular floor-covering and plastic sheeting as used in the packaging industry. I tried to interrupt, but Spot's cries were too loud.

"Listen . . . Murderer . . . Are you . . . Do you really think . . ."

The Murderer ignored me. He had already started digging into my brother The Scotsman's shoulder with a Ryobi EBS-1310 woodworking belt sander.

I had forgotten the Murderer's name.

"Jim . . . Jake . . . Hieronymous . . . You . . . I think you've proved your point. You're a bloody good murderer. You've committed the crimes you were punished for. Isn't it time we got out of here before someone raises the alarm?"

"That wasn't the agreement," said the Murderer, firing up an ergonomically-designed Bosch sabre saw. "The agreement was that we'd commit our crimes and go back to the clink as real criminals."

"I've been having second thoughts," I said. "Not just about the punishment, but about the crime."

"It's a bit late for that," said the Murderer, tossing the Bosch aside and picking up a peach-coloured Silverline impact shredder with dual cutting blades and a safety cut-off switch.

At that moment, Peter and Luisa appeared from behind the felt drapes. I ran over to my children and took them by the hand.

"Let's get out of here," I said.

We exited the glass house, followed by the Murderer, brandishing a Makita petrol hole-borer featuring electronic ignition, hands-free usage, and ultra-low vibration.

39

I remember quite clearly the day when things reached their absolute nadir. It was the day Dad asked me to come and help him at his job.

I didn't even know he had one. It turned out he was working as a janitor at a local school. We both dressed in brown janitor's housecoats and set off.

It was an odd, boxy building, a sort of mid-1960s utopian structure with big windows expressing optimistic idealism and openness. Despite the windows, it was dark inside. My father led me to the janitor's room, which was full of mops and pails. He cleared space on a pink-topped table and chopped out a line of coke, rolled two big spliffs, and prepared some heroin with a candle and spoon.

"Do you want a cup of tea?" my father asked.

"Okay," I said. He switched the kettle on. The drugs were evidently for somebody else.

There came a knock at the door. My father ran over and opened it. There sat a little girl in a wheelchair, pretty as a picture, wearing a flouncy white lace dress. Both her feet were missing.

"Daisy!" Dad exclaimed, lifting her out of the chair and smothering her in kisses. He set her carefully back down in the chair and wheeled her in.

My father lit the two spliffs, handed one to Daisy and puffed on the other himself. He slid the cup of tea roughly across the table to me.

Dad rolled up a banknote and gave it to Daisy. She snorted the coke. Then, anaesthetizing a patch of her skin with a cotton swab, my father injected the heroin into her arm. They gazed smiling into each other's eyes. They were obviously very much in love.

"Dad, I'm going to do the rounds, see if there's any need for a janitor," I said. It was a lie; I just couldn't stay there a moment longer. The sight of my father's new girlfriend sickened me.

I went for a long walk through the school corridors. In the bathroom I stood for a while watching a plumber and his mate, obviously his son, fixing a blocked toilet which had flooded the whole room with a rising tide of brown, shitty water. The father would surface for a spanner, gulp some breath, then disappear deep into the swill. His son, meanwhile, lolled in the doorway, smoking and attempting to chat with me about trivialities.

I was disgusted.

"With an attitude like that you'll never be a success like your dad," I told him, nodding at the brown-faced man.

I continued on my journey through the corridors. A little boy ran up to me.

"The janitor is a pervert!" he said.

"Did you say that knowing that I'm the janitor's son?" I asked.

"No," said the boy. "Do you know who I am?" he asked.

"What does that matter, as long as what you tell me is true?" I said.

"Go on," said the boy, "ask me who I am!"

"Who are you?" I said.

"I'm the uncle of your nephew," said the boy, and ran off.

I came to a classroom. An exam was being held. The invigilator, seeing me in the doorway, gestured me urgently over. His legs were clamped shut.

"I'm dying for a pee," he said, "could you take over for five minutes?"

"All right," I said, "but don't use the bathroom down the hall, it's knee-deep in shit."

"Did you tell me that knowing it's the only one?" asked the invigilator, running off.

I took my place behind the high desk and picked up the examination paper. It was titled "Ethics."

Suddenly I looked up and saw a boy plainly cheating. He was examining the conscience of the boy next to him.

I pretended not to notice, sitting at the high table, folding a sheet of A4 into a paper plane.

"Everything okay?" asked the invigilator when he returned. The cuffs of his trousers were smeared with shit.

"Actually, no," I said, trying not to pay attention to the foul odour. "I caught a boy cheating on the Ethics paper. He was examining the conscience of the boy next to him."

"Which boy was it?"

"That boy over there."

We walked over and stood behind the two boys in question. From the cheat's point of view, his neighbour's conscience could indeed be seen clearly.

Like a landscape viewed from a lighthouse or the tiny scene in a snowstorm paperweight, everything in the luminous, transparent boy was laid out in tiny, familiar clarity. There was the glass house, and there the villa where Joan was living with Joan. A little further away was the hill where I'd met the scary clown, and the place where I'd driven Dad's car over the hill. Everything in the boy was a three-dimensional model of itself. I calculated the scale at 1:32.

It was a snowy day in the boy's conscience. There were flashes of sunshine on copper domes, troikas pulled by reindeer, and tiny electric locomotives tugging luxury carriages through white fields. An ancient brass trumpet sounded and the copper sun began to sink behind the mountains of Summerisle.

My fingers froze to the rim of the railing, and the enormous lamp hummed behind me, its shutter whirring past with the delicacy of a mechanical bird. I began to dream of the relationships I would have with the artists I loved; the opera singer Ludovico, the Modernist Karl Pop, the cabaret satirist Keith Beith.

"Don't worry, I'll take care of this matter," said the invigilator.

I walked back to the janitor's office and paused at the door. Pressing my ear to the wooden panel, I heard nothing. I pushed the door open.

Inside my father was on his knees, sitting on the table. Daisy lay on her tummy, the stumps at the end of her legs pink as butcher's meat. They were both naked. My father's hands were greased yellow and he was massaging Daisy's buttocks.

Daisy was toying with a pile of white powder, sniffing it through an extraordinarily long thin black tube.

Dad looked up, his gaze meeting mine with a calmness that was almost obscene.

"The doctor told Daisy to stay away from cocaine," he explained, "so I bought her a two metre straw."

40

On the run from the Murderer with Peter and Luisa, I began to experience some of the happiest days of my life. Certainly, a maniac was on our trail. Certainly, we might be laid waste at any moment by a flailing pair of Trico windshield wipers with zinc die-cast heads. But, within these conditions, even in the shadow of harm, life became sweet, precious and harmonious.

It so happened that the Architecture Biennial was on in Venice. I decided to take the children to see it, and booked flights. We stayed in a small self-catering apartment on the Fondamenta de la Misericordia. The first morning, sitting with the windows and shutters flung open, and watery sunshine flooding a table spread with an improvised breakfast—panettone, bananas and Twinings English Breakfast tea lightened with synthetic coffee creamer—I felt for once like a real father; normal, kind, decent, adventurous, instructive, fun to be with. Why couldn't life always have been like this?

The three of us set off towards the Giardini, taking labyrinthine backstreets, which, Peter said, reminded him of one of the more beautiful levels of *Tomb Raider*. Venice certainly felt as though it were being continuously, randomly generated by some kind of computer graphics engine. Even the light on the chalky green canals glinted as though someone had spent hours running the effect through filters.

Inside the national pavilions at the Giardini, things were even more gamelike. Everything seemed intended to appeal to a visitor's inner child; there were quarter-scale models of buildings, freestanding structures made of cards, doll's house cafés, wattle huts you could remove your shoes and climb into, a treetop teahouse that swayed gently in the breeze. The children loved it, and I felt more and more like a child myself; after the wattle hut I put my shoes into my bag and padded around the site in my stockinged feet. It felt refreshing.

My hopes that we had left the Murderer far behind began to recede, however, when I started noticing a solitary man on the edge of certain rooms, or a few metres behind us as we crossed the open spaces between pavilions. He wore a broad-brimmed straw hat pulled low over his face and seemed to be avoiding everyone's gaze. He looked like a thresher, a migrant farm worker, a homeless person, an Australian, a backpacker.

I couldn't be sure the Thresher was my old friend the Murderer (it was hard now to believe that we'd so recently been allies and even collaborators), but his spidery presence at the edge of various rooms began to trouble me. What was in that rucksack? How come he was even allowed to carry it in here?

In my stockinged feet I padded over to one of the exhibition guards.

"Excuse me," I asked, "I wonder if you can tell me whether that gentleman . . ."—I turned to point him out, but the

Thresher had disappeared—". . . whether someone would be permitted, under your regulations, to walk around the site with a rucksack on his back?"

The guard explained to me that normally the answer would be no, but that this gentleman might have press accreditation and be carrying, for instance, a bag full of cameras and tripods on his back. He assured me that if he saw the man again he would ask to see his credentials.

I smiled with sarcastic incredulity. "His credentials, I see." Why couldn't he have just come right out and said "testicles"?

In the Japanese pavilion we received a pleasant surprise. One of the officials told us that, owing to a last-minute cancellation, several places had become available on an imminent tour of an exhibition celebrating the buildings of Atelier Bow Wow. Quarter-scale models of the team's structures had been assembled at the Venice Zoo.

"The children will love it!" I exclaimed. All that mattered to me now was their happiness.

The staff in the Japanese Pavilion explained to us that a model of Atelier Bow Wow's Palette House—which actually stood in Karita-gun, Miyagi Prefecture—had been constructed in the Penguin House at the zoo. The team's 1992 Kiosk for Vegetables now stood beside the shed housing the zoo's woolly alpacas. Their Moth House in Miyota now stood next to the zoo's Insect House. The Black Dog House they had built in Nagano rose amid a prairie housing wild dogs. The Juicy House, from Setagaya-ku, Tokyo, was reconstructed in every detail inside the Camel House, which had been renamed for the occasion "the Juicy Camel House." And their famous Kusasenri Toilet—a rough pine-clad, grass-roofed urinal on the highway outside Aso in Kumamoto Prefecture—had been built at quarter scale next to the zoo's own toilets, confusing many members of the public, who had to crawl on hands and knees through the entrance to pee.

The only trouble is, the Japanese Pavilion staff were also offering a free place on this fascinating architectural tour to the frightening Thresher, who materialized from the shadows just as the exhibition was being described to us, and couldn't very well be left out.

We were all led to the same water taxi. It was impossible to refuse. The driver helped the Thresher into the boat, taking the weight of the Makita BHX2500 high-performance leaf blower while the gaunt, stooped man found his feet in the boat.

"It's a beautiful tool, Signor!" marveled the boatman.

"Thank you," said the Murderer (for it was clearly him), raising his straw brim. "The new 4-stroke engine runs on unleaded fuel, is much quieter than a 2-stroke, has lower emissions and—with twin bearing cast-steel crank and chrome bore—is ideal for durability, performance and long life."

"Will you be requiring it during the journey?" asked the boatman.

"Yes," said the Murderer.

41

Starlight streamed into our glass house just before dawn on the morning of my fifteenth birthday.

"Ask me for anything you want," said my father, "and it's yours. I swear it by the river by which the adults take their oaths—the river of Styx which my eyes have never seen. Let those sacred waters be witness to my promise."

I had no idea what he was talking about, or why his tone was so highfalutin. But I did understand that my father was offering me anything I wanted, and swearing he'd give it to me.

"I want to drive your car," I said.

My father blanched. I could see immediately that he regretted his oath.

"Shit," he said, "I was afraid you'd say that. That's the very last thing I want to give you. I can't back out of my promise now, but I can try to talk you out of it."

"What you're asking to do is fucking dangerous," continued Dad. "It's a major, major privilege, and you're just not old or strong or experienced enough to drive that car. It just isn't for teenagers. Even among adults, I'm the only one who's allowed to drive my car. However pleased with themselves those adults—friends of mine—might be as far as their skills at driving their own cars, when it comes to driving mine they're stumped. Useless."

Dad was pacing up and down the breakfast room, gesticulating, making driving gestures.

"Even your grandfather the bus driver couldn't drive my car, and nobody's a better driver than he was. The thing is, as soon as you get it out onto the road and switch the headlights on you're going to have to climb the hill. If you stall you'll roll back down and probably veer out of control. Even a glance in the rear-view mirror might give you vertigo and make you panic. I panic myself at the top of that hill. My mouth goes dry, my heart hammers."

My father mimed gripping a wheel, a hammy expression of livid terror on his face.

"Then you've got to drive down the other side. You've got to grip the steering wheel incredibly tightly on that descent. Heaven forbid it should be raining or icy! On rainy days I see old Bob Tethys, who lives on the hill there, standing in his doorway, genuinely afraid for me on my descent. You've got to think of the sky, too—it's turning, whirling in circles above your head, so fast you get dizzy. I tend to grit my teeth and just drive on, trying to ignore the spinning sky occupying so much of the windscreen. But it's bloody difficult.

"You probably think you're in for a pleasant trip along a suburban street. But all sorts of dangers await you. Supposing I do give you the car this morning, how will you stop your own headlights from dazzling you? How will you steel the machine against the constant influence of the magnetic poles, or hold it steady under the careering sky? What if there's a meteor shower and you get hit? And think of all the terrifying animals up there in the stars, those fierce astrological signs waiting to tear you limb from limb! The scorpion, the lion, the Thracian archer!"

"What the hell are you talking about, Dad?" I said, getting angry. "Just give me the fucking keys! You promised!"

"No, no, think about it, ask for something—anything—else!" said Dad, so pale he lit the whole house like a silver photographic reflector. It was getting uncomfortably bright in there.

"I'm only saying this because I care for you, and because I really am your Dad," said Dad. It was an odd thing to declare. I flared up.

"You're fucking with my head, Dad," I said. "First you say I can have anything, then when I name something you say not that. I'm perfectly capable of driving the car. I've done it a million times in video games. I've told you what I want for my birthday, and I'm sticking by it. Let me drive the car. All your stupid bullshit warnings have just made me more eager and more determined to show I can do it."

Dad was positively incandescent, but a promise was a promise. He led me through the side door to the glass garage. We gazed at the six-litre Vulcan in awe. The axles and transmission shaft were pure gold. The wheels had golden hub caps and silver spokes. Chrysolites and diamonds studded the bodywork.

As I stood there admiring the sweet machine, the horns of the vanishing moon faded from sight, and far in the crimsoning east wakeful dawn threw wide the shining doors of her rose-filled chambers. While the stars fled, the morning star shepherding their long columns, I snatched the keys from Dad, got in and switched the Vulcan on. The motor rumbled and rattled into life and the garage was filled with the distinct smell of ambrosia.

Dad tried to rub some Lavera SPF40 sunscreen into my face, but I pushed him away. "Fuck off!"

I was my own man.

I flicked on the dazzling headlights and pulled out of the garage, Dad's words of advice fading in the roaring of the engine. "Watch out for the speed bumps! Grip the wheel firmly! Press lightly on the accelerator! Take the curved road over the hill, not the straight one! Aim midway between the serpent and the altar!"

It really wasn't like driving a car in a computer game. I was surprised at how difficult it was to keep control. The car leapt forward as if expecting a much heavier passenger. I panicked. The wheel beneath my hands seemed to have a life of its own; it twisted this way and that. We were already on the wrong road, and the wildly raking headlights seemed to set everything they touched on fire. I couldn't control my legs, they were trembling so much.

The earth was on fire, trees were ash, cities fell. My hair was full of cinders, the Vulcan was white hot. Suddenly the road seemed carpeted by scorpions. Nothing but scorpions from verge to verge! My hands fell from the wheel, and we seemed to rush between the trees and far into the air. The moon was below us and the clouds were smoke.

At that moment, Zeus, father of the gods, loomed enormous, filling the whole windscreen and brandishing in his hand a live, writhing filament of lightning. He hurled the thunderbolt and the Vulcan exploded. I fell earthwards with my hair on fire. People on the ground thought I was a shooting star. The river of Eridanus received me with a great gulp, extinguishing the fire in my hair and pulling me down to its depths. As I began to lose consciousness, I saw the remains of the burning car plummeting towards the earth and heard the booming voice of my father.

"I told you so," he said, and caught me in his arms.

42

I didn't even know Venice had a zoo. As the water taxi scuds through the waves of the lagoon I approach the driver to ask him where we're heading. He gestures vaguely towards an island far out along the archipelago.

The Murderer skulks at the back of the boat, eyeing my children and oiling his Makita BHX2500 high-performance leaf blower. He unsettles me deeply, but I'm determined not to make any contact with the man—to act, in fact, as if he were not there. Peter and Luisa, meanwhile, amuse themselves picking apart a brine shrimp they've found on the wooden seat. I want to point out the fascinating lack of a cephalothorax, the ventral thoracopods, but I know the children won't listen. They're playing the Spanish Inquisition and the shrimp is a heretic.

Suddenly we begin to skid in a slalom zigzag, narrowly missing the marker buoys and danger signs that punctuate the main traffic route across the lagoon. Realising that the taxi driver has fallen asleep at the wheel, I hurry up to the front and shake the man by the shoulder.

"When my time comes to go," I say, trying to make light of the situation in order to spare the driver's feelings, "I want to die peacefully in my sleep like you, not screaming in terror like the rest of us were just now!"

Rather than laughing, the driver scowls, signals me to sit down, then picks up his intercom and radios ahead to the island—some brief message in Italian I can't understand.

Eventually we reach the island, Santa Francesco. Palm trees and an assortment of architectural follies in exotic styles mark the location of the zoo.

"How are those three arseholes of yours?" the dockhand calls to the taxi driver as he moors the vessel. I turn to the children.

"Remind me never again to ride in a water taxi piloted by a man with three arseholes," I say, loud enough for the taxi driver to hear.

"If you three don't ride with me I won't have three arseholes," the driver spits back.

The Murderer, drifting behind us, cackles and revs his leaf blower. I can contain my irritation no longer. I turn and shout at him:

"Can't you shut that thing off?"

"Are you scared?" the Murderer asks, tauntingly. "Does my leaf blower frighten you?"

"Scared?" I retort promptly, "I'm not the one who's going to have to go back across this lagoon alone!"

The Murderer drops back into the shadows, skulking along behind us.

"I want an ice cream!" cries Luisa. She's spotted a cart by the zoo gates.

"You don't want an ice cream now," I tell her, "we're about to see some exciting animals! And architecture!"

"Dad, I don't want to see animals or architecture, I want to eat ice cream!"

I try to distract her.

"Luisa, let's play a game!"

"What game?"

"The Spanish Inquisition!" shouts Peter.

"No," says Luisa, "we've already played that. Let's play Daddies and Mummies!"

"All right, Daddies and Mummies," I say. "Who are you?"

"I'm the Mummy," says Luisa.

"And what do you want me to do?" I ask.

"You're the Daddy. Undress and go and lie down on that bench over there."

I do as she asks. The bench is next to the ice cream cart. The vendor looks at my naked body suspiciously.

Presently Luisa arrives. She's also naked.

"Now what, Luisa?"

"Buy your daughter an ice cream!" commands Luisa, in a voice remarkably like her mother's.

"Yes, and your son too," adds Peter, also in his mother's voice. He's also naked.

"You'll find the money in my trouser pocket," I tell the children. "Over there."

Luisa runs off to get the cash. The ice cream vendor looks at us with stupefied contempt, but hands over three fresh ice-cream cones. The smooth, cold vanilla fluff is delicious.

The architectural tour guide runs over from the gate of the zoo. He's Japanese, and seems too polite to notice that we're naked.

"You are the Biennial party? Walk this way."

Peter and Luisa immediately begin to copy his amusing style of walking. I give Peter a warning slap on the head.

The guide leads us to the Penguin House, where a quarter-scale replica of Atelier Bow Wow's Palette House now stands. The children are allowed to play in it. Next it's the Alpaca compound, where the foolish, woolly animals tug at turnips poking out of Bow Wow's Kiosk for Vegetables. Peter and Luisa pet them while I watch, smiling. At the Juicy Camel House Luisa suddenly announces that she needs to pee, and I carry her on my shoulders to the rough pine-clad, grass-roofed urinal near the aviary. It's so small we have to crawl in on our hands and knees.

The exotic duck compound is next to the toilet building. I'm just pointing out to Peter and Luisa the exquisite plumage of a pair of mating Smew when I hear the horrible sound of the Murderer's Makita BHX2500 high-performance leaf blower starting up directly behind us.

"I'm going to kill you and your whole family," says the Murderer.

I walk away from the joke my father is telling. I've never had much of a stomach for violence, and anyway, the punchline can surely wait a couple of minutes.

I stroll to the brink of the lagoon, which isn't far away. The water slops and slaps against the stone embankment, and intense highlights of misty sun bob and fizzle on the waves. Little boats are scudding to and fro on the surface of the slate-grey water, plying their way back and forth between the zoo and the domes, spires, towers and palazzi of Venice.

The thought occurs to me that whatever happens to us now, the city will still be here after the joke is done—this bizarre, beautiful, tendentious labyrinth built on alder pilings, oak planks, and marble slabs. Then I remember that Dad has told us that Venice is slipping into the water, down towards the silt and mud it was built on. But—and this is important—it's happening very, very slowly.

The darting water craft remind me of hemiptera—the water striders I'd watch with Dad on Summerisle, scooting along the surface of ponds using only the water's surface tension to support them. Dad once made me learn the names of the insects' leg segments: the coxa, the trochanter, the femur, the tibia and the tarsus.

"The coxa, the trochanter, the femur, the tibia and the tarsus," I recite, walking back towards the joke, where the punchline is now imminent.

Before he can point the Makita at us, the Murderer is startled by the rattling wings of a Meller's Yellow Bill, swooping down at him from behind. In the resulting confusion the barrel of the leaf blower is turned directly into the Thresher's own face, which blows off up into the sky.

The Murderer falls to the ground. He doesn't seem to be breathing, and his eyes are rolled back in his featureless head.

"Call emergency services!" shouts a Northern Mallard.

"Yes," squawks a Narrow-Billed Harlequin Pochard, "call the hospital!"

A Ruddy Masked Brazilian Teal whips out a phone.

"We have a human here who's dead," the duck reports, "what should we do?"

The operator, in a calm, soothing voice, says: "Now, just take it easy, I'm here to help. First, let's make sure he's dead."

There's a silence, then the harsh rasp of the Makita leaf blower engine fills the afternoon for a few seconds.

"Fucking typical," moans what's left of the Murderer. He dies.

The Teal comes back on the line. "Okay," it says, "now what?"

"Yes," echoes a Salvadori's Freckled Torrent Duck, "now what?"

And all the other exotic ducks take up the refrain. "Now what? Now what?"

It sounds like the honking squall of a laughtrack.

Just then I see a goddess approaching in diaphanous gauze. I recognise my wife and mother, Joan. She wears a breathtaking diplax hymation and electric green mantile in Thracian style.

I am overjoyed.

"These are the pigs I've been fucking!" I exclaim, throwing my arms around Peter, Luisa and my father.

Joan smiles. "Those aren't pigs," she says, sweeping the loose fabric of the hymation over her shoulder, "they're our family!"

And, clustered together like one animal rather than four, we embrace, our collective face wet with tears.

"We weren't speaking to you," we say, speaking to you.

Momus, (aka Nick Currie) was born in Scotland in 1960. The son of a linguist, he began a career as a singer-songwriter in London in the mid-'80s, and has since released twenty albums of songs in styles ranging from chamber pop to exuberant folktronica, as well as working as an artist, and a journalist for *Wired*, *The New York Times*, and many other publications.

SELECTED DALKEY ARCHIVE PAPERBACKS

PETROS ABATZOGLOU, *What Does Mrs. Freeman Want?*
MICHAL AJVAZ, *The Other City.*
PIERRE ALBERT-BIROT, *Grabinoulor.*
YUZ ALESHKOVSKY, *Kangaroo.*
FELIPE ALFAU, *Chromos.*
   Locos.
IVAN ÂNGELO, *The Celebration.*
   The Tower of Glass.
DAVID ANTIN, *Talking.*
ANTÓNIO LOBO ANTUNES, *Knowledge of Hell.*
ALAIN ARIAS-MISSON, *Theatre of Incest.*
JOHN ASHBERY AND JAMES SCHUYLER, *A Nest of Ninnies.*
HEIMRAD BÄCKER, *transcript.*
DJUNA BARNES, *Ladies Almanack.*
   Ryder.
JOHN BARTH, *LETTERS.*
   Sabbatical.
DONALD BARTHELME, *The King.*
   Paradise.
SVETISLAV BASARA, *Chinese Letter.*
MARK BINELLI, *Sacco and Vanzetti Must Die!*
ANDREI BITOV, *Pushkin House.*
LOUIS PAUL BOON, *Chapel Road.*
   My Little War.
   Summer in Termuren.
ROGER BOYLAN, *Killoyle.*
IGNÁCIO DE LOYOLA BRANDÃO, *Anonymous Celebrity.*
   Teeth under the Sun.
   Zero.
BONNIE BREMSER, *Troia: Mexican Memoirs.*
CHRISTINE BROOKE-ROSE, *Amalgamemnon.*
BRIGID BROPHY, *In Transit.*
MEREDITH BROSNAN, *Mr. Dynamite.*
GERALD L. BRUNS, *Modern Poetry and
   the Idea of Language.*
EVGENY BUNIMOVICH AND J. KATES, EDS.,
   Contemporary Russian Poetry: An Anthology.
GABRIELLE BURTON, *Heartbreak Hotel.*
MICHEL BUTOR, *Degrees.*
   Mobile.
   Portrait of the Artist as a Young Ape.
G. CABRERA INFANTE, *Infante's Inferno.*
   Three Trapped Tigers.
JULIETA CAMPOS, *The Fear of Losing Eurydice.*
ANNE CARSON, *Eros the Bittersweet.*
CAMILO JOSÉ CELA, *Christ versus Arizona.*
   The Family of Pascual Duarte.
   The Hive.
LOUIS-FERDINAND CÉLINE, *Castle to Castle.*
   Conversations with Professor Y.
   London Bridge.
   Normance.
   North.
   Rigadoon.
HUGO CHARTERIS, *The Tide Is Right.*
JEROME CHARYN, *The Tar Baby.*
MARC CHOLODENKO, *Mordechai Schamz.*
EMILY HOLMES COLEMAN, *The Shutter of Snow.*
ROBERT COOVER, *A Night at the Movies.*
STANLEY CRAWFORD, *Log of the S.S. The Mrs Unguentine.*
   Some Instructions to My Wife.
ROBERT CREELEY, *Collected Prose.*
RENÉ CREVEL, *Putting My Foot in It.*
RALPH CUSACK, *Cadenza.*
SUSAN DAITCH, *L.C.*
   Storytown.
NICHOLAS DELBANCO, *The Count of Concord.*
NIGEL DENNIS, *Cards of Identity.*
PETER DIMOCK, *A Short Rhetoric for Leaving the Family.*
ARIEL DORFMAN, *Konfidenz.*
COLEMAN DOWELL, *The Houses of Children.*
   Island People.
   Too Much Flesh and Jabez.
ARKADII DRAGOMOSHCHENKO, *Dust.*
RIKKI DUCORNET, *The Complete Butcher's Tales.*
   The Fountains of Neptune.
   The Jade Cabinet.
   The One Marvelous Thing.
   Phosphor in Dreamland.
   The Stain.
   The Word "Desire."
WILLIAM EASTLAKE, *The Bamboo Bed.*
   Castle Keep.
   Lyric of the Circle Heart.
JEAN ECHENOZ, *Chopin's Move.*
STANLEY ELKIN, *A Bad Man.*
   Boswell: A Modern Comedy.
   Criers and Kibitzers, Kibitzers and Criers.
   The Dick Gibson Show.
   The Franchiser.
   George Mills.
   The Living End.
   The MacGuffin.
   The Magic Kingdom.
   Mrs. Ted Bliss.
   The Rabbi of Lud.
   Van Gogh's Room at Arles.
ANNIE ERNAUX, *Cleaned Out.*
LAUREN FAIRBANKS, *Muzzle Thyself.*
   Sister Carrie.
JUAN FILLOY, *Op Oloop.*
LESLIE A. FIEDLER, *Love and Death in the American Novel.*

GUSTAVE FLAUBERT, *Bouvard and Pécuchet.*
KASS FLEISHER, *Talking out of School.*
FORD MADOX FORD, *The March of Literature.*
JON FOSSE, *Melancholy.*
MAX FRISCH, *I'm Not Stiller.*
   Man in the Holocene.
CARLOS FUENTES, *Christopher Unborn.*
   Distant Relations.
   Terra Nostra.
   Where the Air Is Clear.
JANICE GALLOWAY, *Foreign Parts.*
   The Trick Is to Keep Breathing.
WILLIAM H. GASS, *Cartesian Sonata and Other Novellas.*
   Finding a Form.
   A Temple of Texts.
   The Tunnel.
   Willie Masters' Lonesome Wife.
GÉRARD GAVARRY, *Hoplla! 1 2 3.*
ETIENNE GILSON, *The Arts of the Beautiful.*
   Forms and Substances in the Arts.
C. S. GISCOMBE, *Giscome Road.*
   Here.
   Prairie Style.
DOUGLAS GLOVER, *Bad News of the Heart.*
   The Enamoured Knight.
WITOLD GOMBROWICZ, *A Kind of Testament.*
KAREN ELIZABETH GORDON, *The Red Shoes.*
GEORGI GOSPODINOV, *Natural Novel.*
JUAN GOYTISOLO, *Count Julian.*
   Juan the Landless.
   Makbara.
   Marks of Identity.
PATRICK GRAINVILLE, *The Cave of Heaven.*
HENRY GREEN, *Back.*
   Blindness.
   Concluding.
   Doting.
   Nothing.
JIŘÍ GRUŠA, *The Questionnaire.*
GABRIEL GUDDING, *Rhode Island Notebook.*
JOHN HAWKES, *Whistlejacket.*
ALEKSANDAR HEMON, ED., *Best European Fiction 2010.*
AIDAN HIGGINS, *A Bestiary.*
   Balcony of Europe.
   Bornholm Night-Ferry.
   Darkling Plain: Texts for the Air.
   Flotsam and Jetsam.
   Langrishe, Go Down.
   Scenes from a Receding Past.
   Windy Arbours.
ALDOUS HUXLEY, *Antic Hay.*
   Crome Yellow.
   Point Counter Point.
   Those Barren Leaves.
   Time Must Have a Stop.
MIKHAIL IOSSEL AND JEFF PARKER, EDS., *Amerika:
   Contemporary Russians View the United States.*
GERT JONKE, *Geometric Regional Novel.*
   Homage to Czerny.
   The System of Vienna.
JACQUES JOUET, *Mountain R.*
   Savage.
CHARLES JULIET, *Conversations with Samuel Beckett and
   Bram van Velde.*
MIEKO KANAI, *The Word Book.*
HUGH KENNER, *The Counterfeiters.*
   Flaubert, Joyce and Beckett: The Stoic Comedians.
   Joyce's Voices.
DANILO KIŠ, *Garden, Ashes.*
   A Tomb for Boris Davidovich.
ANITA KONKKA, *A Fool's Paradise.*
GEORGE KONRÁD, *The City Builder.*
TADEUSZ KONWICKI, *A Minor Apocalypse.*
   The Polish Complex.
MENIS KOUMANDAREAS, *Koula.*
ELAINE KRAF, *The Princess of 72nd Street.*
JIM KRUSOE, *Iceland.*
EWA KURYLUK, *Century 21.*
ERIC LAURRENT, *Do Not Touch.*
VIOLETTE LEDUC, *La Bâtarde.*
SUZANNE JILL LEVINE, *The Subversive Scribe:
   Translating Latin American Fiction.*
DEBORAH LEVY, *Billy and Girl.*
   Pillow Talk in Europe and Other Places.
JOSÉ LEZAMA LIMA, *Paradiso.*
ROSA LIKSOM, *Dark Paradise.*
OSMAN LINS, *Avalovara.*
   The Queen of the Prisons of Greece.
ALF MAC LOCHLAINN, *The Corpus in the Library.*
   Out of Focus.
RON LOEWINSOHN, *Magnetic Field(s).*
BRIAN LYNCH, *The Winner of Sorrow.*
D. KEITH MANO, *Take Five.*
MICHELINE AHARONIAN MARCOM, *The Mirror in the Well.*
BEN MARCUS, *The Age of Wire and String.*
WALLACE MARKFIELD, *Teitlebaum's Window.*
   To an Early Grave.
DAVID MARKSON, *Reader's Block.*
   Springer's Progress.
   Wittgenstein's Mistress.
CAROLE MASO, *AVA.*

FOR A FULL LIST OF PUBLICATIONS, VISIT:
www.dalkeyarchive.com

SELECTED DALKEY ARCHIVE PAPERBACKS

FOR A FULL LIST OF PUBLICATIONS, VISIT:
www.dalkeyarchive.com